COYOTE
JUSTICE

A Novella by

K E R I   M I L L S

PAGE PUBLISHING, INC.
Conneaut Lake, PA

First originally published by Page Publishing 2019

ISBN 978-1-68456-744-7 (pbk)
ISBN 978-1-68456-745-4 (digital)

Printed in the United States of America

DEDICATION

For my wonderful nieces and nephews, Alison, Jamie, Mallory, Preston, Aaron and Ryan. Keep me on your bookshelf forever as you are forever in my heart!

ACKNOWLEDGEMENTS

Special thanks to my best and dearest friend Jane for listening to my crazy ideas, giving me more and supporting my work on this book, and to my fellow author and great cowboy friend Joe Jessup for making me dig deeper and let my imagination run wild.

PROLOGUE

The windowless white panel van sped east on 145 toward Dolores, Colorado, its cargo, four young women. Talib, a small, angry-looking, dark-eyed man at the wheel, was charged with delivering these girls to the rendezvous point deep in the mountains of Montezuma County. From there, the girls would be transferred to a second vehicle and transported to the casino in Ignacio, a small town on the New Mexico border. He gripped the wheel tightly as the road wound and curved. It was raining furiously, and the windshield wipers fought in vain to clear the glass. They would have to stop and wait out the storm and then continue the few hours left to the transfer point. A few miles up the road, he saw the Dolores riverboat launch sign and pulled in. The wind had broken a large limb from a ponderosa tree across the drive, and debris was scattered everywhere, but he could clearly see a couple of porta johns, a handwashing station, and a registration box at the head of a wide, muddy trail that led to the river below. This would be the perfect stop. He was ready for an interlude with his favorite of the four prostitutes in his charge. After all, it may be weeks before she was recycled back to his territory in Nevada.

He pulled the van up to the porta johns, turned off the vehicle and grabbed Consuela, the youngest of the women, sixteen at best, by the hair and pulled her to the front of the van. Forcing her to kneel, he dropped his pants and pulled her into his lap, holding the gun barrel against her temple. His groans of ecstasy brought bile to the throats of the three women in the back, while Consuela choked and stared at the floor. In the darkness, Consuela saw a faint glint of some object at Talib's feet. She slid her hand across the floorboard and grasped the tiny key lying just outside of the crumpled jeans around Talib's ankles, and she quietly slipped it into her pocket. Talib finished with a grunt and gave her a violent shove, pulled up his pants, and hissed, "Get in the back and shut up."

Half an hour passed, and the rain began to let up. All four girls needed to relieve themselves, and for that matter, he could too. He pulled his gun, opened the side panel of the vehicle, and the girls poured out of the van.

Of the four captives, Consuela Rodriguez was a strong-willed, independent fighter who saw this stop as an opportunity to escape. She quickly assessed the scene and saw her weapon. A broken limb with a razor-sharp point lay at her feet. Talib, back turned to her, was shoving another of the young women into the john when Consuela struck with a vicious swing to his head and a violent stab into his hamstring. Talib screamed in pain. "Run!" Consuela yelled, and the four girls ran wildly down the slippery trail and found themselves at the river's edge. There were a half-dozen rubber rafts moored and loaded with gear on the shore, waiting for a commercial river trip scheduled to launch the next morning, but with the storm the launch site was void of people. They could hear Talib cursing and sliding down the trail behind them. Terrified, Consuela untied one of the rafts, shoved the three others into the raft, pushed off into the river, and headed blindly downstream in the raging current.

CHAPTER ONE

Ben Doogan, local rancher and retired Montezuma county sheriff, pulled his rig up the road toward the north gate of his sprawling three-thousand-acre ranch. The remaining snow was melting fast, and muddy water raced down the tire tracks, making both truck and trailer slip and slide as it continued up the final incline to the locked entrance. He stopped the vehicle and stepped out. He smiled as he admired the impressive iron gate that proudly displayed his "3 Bar D" brand perfectly welded in the center. The massive structure was held secure by opposing slate-rock pillars carefully laid, blending into the surroundings as if nature herself had built them. In fact, these stone pillars had been lovingly built by him, his widow Gina, and young daughter Jess, the "3 D's" themselves, with each stone hand-picked and placed. He smiled again as he gazed at the three hand-prints embedded in the mortar and the fingerprinted date, 1985. They had built a beautiful gate and a life together, and Ben would always be grateful for that. He had served the county for thirty years, and when he lost his Gina twenty-five years earlier, killed by a drunk driver, he raised their only child, Jess, on his own in the only way he knew how. He and Jess rode the range, tending to his five-hun-dred-head herd of black Angus cattle. They spent summers together at weekend rodeos, team roping and team penning. The two were inseparable, and Jess learned every roping trick in the book from her dad. The local rod-and-gun club was also no stranger to either Jess or Ben, and they were the envy of every marksman for the speed, accu-racy, and perfection brought to every shot. Ben's fireplace mantle was covered in trophies from the hundreds of competitions that Jess won.

Trick shooting, skeet shooting, target shooting, every category and every firearm. For a single dad, he had done all right at least on the cowboy'n side, and Jess was the envy of all the young men who paled in comparison in that arena. Ben did get a little feminine help raising Jess from Gina's sister Caroline, a registered nurse who lived in Denver. Jess would spend every spring break up north with her aunt, where she would get to go to the salons, get manicures and massages, go shopping for pretty clothes, and talk about…what? Well, hell, he didn't know what girls talked about. He just knew that every time his little girl came home from a trip to Caroline's, she looked prettier than when she left. Seemed like yesterday when Jess was that little girl helping him on the ranch, and now she was a grown-up lady with a college degree in forensic science and medicine from the University of New Mexico. She had chosen to come home to Echo to work and was the acting medical examiner for the county.

He would have welcomed her help today with the cattle as a violent spring rain in the San Juan Mountains had caused massive flash flooding in the high country, and his cows were starting to calve. He needed to get them back down to the ranch before a second wave of storms stranded the herd. As he unloaded his big gelding, Hank, from the trailer, his two hired hands, Pedro Juarez and Gavin McCallen, arrived on horseback up from the draw.

"There is a lot of area washed out just north of here," said Gavin, "but I think if we ride up the east slope, we can get around it. We saw fifteen head on the side of the wash, and my guess is the rest headed up to higher ground." Ben nodded, and they set out on the trail.

As they rounded a grove of Aspen trees, Hank snorted and stopped short. Vultures were circling above, and a murder of crows sounded the alarm of their trespass. Pedro was the first to see a splash of bright red under the thin veil of water ahead in the creek bed as it poured over the rocks.

"Señor, hay algo en el agua!" exclaimed Pedro.

Ben's face paled as he moved closer. "It is a body! Looks like a woman."

A rush of memory flooded over Ben as he watched the icy water carving scarlet ribbons across her back and pushing her long black hair into the current over the rocks. His wife, Gina, had been hit and killed by a drunk driver twenty-five years ago while she was changing a flat tire on her car. Ben was the first responder at the crash site. The impact had knocked her facedown thirty yards and into an irrigation ditch filled with water. *Stay focused*

"Gavin, go back down to the truck and call the sheriff. There is no signal up here. Tell him to hurry!"

"Yes, sir!" said Gavin, turning and galloping back down the mountain.

Ben turned and saw his hired hand staring wide-eyed at the body. "Pedro, don't touch anything," Ben said softly.

How on earth did this little gal get here? This is crazy.

CHAPTER TWO

A log snapped in the fire, and the faint hint of burning cedar floated carelessly into the room. Jess Doogan pulled the quilt up tight around her neck and slowly drifted back to sleep, when the silence of the early dawn was pierced by the shrieking wails of a large pack of coyotes, triumphant in their hunt. There was a chill in the air, and the sunrise shivered as it watched the feast below. Jess shuddered, knowing the violence that ravaged the prey, when her cell phone blasted an alarm, shooting her straight up in bed with a start!

"Jess, it's Sheriff Martin. We just got a call from your dad's hired hand out on his north range. They found a body in Echo Creek, a woman. She appears to be native but is facedown, and they won't touch the body until we get a team up there. Grab your gear and meet me at the office."

"A woman!" she exclaimed. "I'll be right there, Sheriff."

As the medical examiner (ME) in the small town of Echo, Colorado, she didn't often get calls like this, and this one smelled of foul play. Jess threw on a pair of jeans and a sweatshirt; pulled her long red hair up under her official ME ball cap; slipped on her cowboy boots; grabbed a jacket, her camera, and forensics bag; and headed out the door. She climbed into her 1970 K20 4x4 fire-engine red Chevy pickup, her pride and joy, which she had traded for her silver Circle Y roping saddle she won at a rodeo and a Winchester Model 70 rifle won at a shooting competition with an aspiring rodeo cowboy short on cash. The engine had needed a little work, but for the value on the trade, she got a great deal. After the tune-up and replacement of worn wires and plugs, Big Red purred like a kitten on the highway and roared like a lion on the rugged terrain of Southwestern Colorado. Jess fired up the truck, made a quick run through the Java Jug drive-through for a double-shot espresso, and pulled up in front of the sheriff's office.

CHAPTER THREE

Sheriff Bodie Martin was a quiet, kind, middle-aged man with a balding head being overrun by a bushy beard climbing up the side of his face. He had served as Montezuma County sheriff deputy to Ben Doogan until Ben's retirement a year ago. Folks in town liked Bodie because he, like Ben, was willing to turn a blind eye to the few minor infractions that were an integral part of the ranching lifestyle. For instance, when a neighbor wasn't using his irrigation turn because the hay was down, another might take the turn without consequence or those occasional deer and elk harvests outside of a hunting season in a harsh winter. All in all, the residents of Echo were hardworking, willing to share with others, and kept to themselves. The only crime that ever seemed to happen in Echo was a minor scrap in Shorty's Bar over a woman. This body up in the creek was a foreign and disconcerting situation, and the fear in Bodie's eyes told me he was as uncomfortable about it as I was.

We gathered up supplies, hooked the ATV trailer to the back of the truck, and drove silently up to the recovery scene.

When we pulled up to the gate on the mountain, my dad was waiting. He had sent Pedro and Gavin home and would worry about getting the cattle tomorrow. Right now there was much to be done, and even though retired, Ben's experience of thirty years in law enforcement would be greatly valued to all of us. We unloaded the ATV and headed up the trail to the creek.

The body was facedown in the water, partially exposed. I began taking pictures from every angle and walked up the creek a short distance, looking for any additional signs of clothing fragments or other evidence that might help tell the story. Nothing. Bodie and Dad carefully lifted the body from the water and laid her gently on the grass while I began making preliminary notations. She was badly bruised and looked to have been in the water for at least twenty-four hours. Liver probe would help estimate a time of death, but first I needed to get her to the mortuary, which was also my lab, and dig deeper. We carefully lifted her onto the rear rack of the ATV and headed down to the truck.

*****

From behind a ponderosa pine about one hundred yards up the creek bed, Talib Akmed removed his satellite phone from his pack and dialed Hassan. "They have one of the girls. She is exactly where you said. I know not which, but she is dead, and they are taking her to Echo for autopsy. What do you want me to do?"

"Follow them, make no more mistakes, and be discreet," Hassan growled.

CHAPTER FOUR

Hassan was a small man with a huge chip on his shoulder from an ugly scar on his face delivered by a vicious attack from a wild boar when he was just a boy in Hawija, a small town north of Mozul in Iraq. His family had immigrated to Russia when he was in his teens, where he was treated as an outcast by peers and suffered years of bullying and ridicule from his deformity. This abuse and humiliation served as the motive for him to become a marksman of extraordinary ability. He was merciless in his aim. Hassan left Russia at twenty-one and illegally entered the United States, hiding in the trunk of a car onboard a cargo ship to Alaska. From there he had worked on fishing boats and found his way to Seattle. It was there where he met "the Doctor."

Angered by the escape of his women and their cargo, Hassan grabbed his .22 Remington rifle and drove out to the mesa. He sat motionless on a rock, scanning the desert and watching as the prairie dogs popped up from their dens and scouted for enemies. As the dogs emerged, he swiftly aimed and blew their faces off, laughing viciously with sick satisfaction.

CHAPTER FIVE

Fogerty's Funeral Home and Furniture Store had been a family business in Echo for nearly seventy-five years. The family who owned it was well respected by the town for providing excellent care of loved ones lost and also providing the community with home furnishings at an affordable price. The building was the largest structure in Echo, with a beautiful chapel and gathering area for families. My office and lab was a nine-hundred-square-foot room in the basement with an embalming table, exam table, computers, mass spectrometer, and a refrigerated vault. Most of all my forensic and autopsy work was done to confirm cause of death. This exam on our victim would prove to be much more comprehensive.

I guess my interest in forensics started when I was a little girl in biology class dissecting frogs. I was intrigued by the connections each organ had to another and the story it told. The same held true when my dad and I would hunt elk. To everyone else, after the kill, it was a gut pile. To me, it was an engineering feat that had no match by mankind in its perfection.

I was only eight years old when my mother was killed by a drunk driver, and the medical examiner at the time was able to determine exactly how much alcohol was in his blood and discovered large amounts of THC in his hair analysis and an unusually high white blood cell count, which confirmed terminal leukemia. His suicide was my mother's murder, and though that brought no comfort to any of the family, it did give us answers, and answers were what I wanted to find for this poor girl lying on my exam table.

I carefully began a close physical exam. You could tell even through the bruised and battered face that she had been stunning. Her olive skin, long, straight, black hair and dark eyes put my first determination of ethnicity to be South American, perhaps Brazilian. I took my scissors and began cutting away her red blouse. It was covered in clay mud from the flash flood. I tossed it into the evidence tray and heard a clink as it hit the metal. I picked up the blouse again and saw a thin gold chain wrapped around a button. It was wound tightly, and I carefully began untangling the knot. It revealed a gold chain with an oval pendant. The name "Consuela" was engraved on the front, and "Com Amor" had been engraved on the back. Portuguese, I was close. "Well now, Consuela, let's find out what happened to you."

When cutting off her brassiere, I found a large deposit of a gray silt-like substance and scraped a good-sized sample into a bag for DNA testing. The results could be an indicator of where she started her swim. The Dolores river bottom was much rockier, and the minerals and nutrients were much different from Echo Creek, which branched from the river about ten miles north and west of where we had found the body.

"Okay, Consuela, what else can you tell me?" I carefully cut her blue jeans down the side seams and pulled them off, letting them fall to the floor as the small key slipped out of her pocket and rested under the wheel of the exam table unnoticed. Looking down at the battered, naked body in front of me, I stared at her midriff. She had a large butterfly tattoo that covered her navel, and the wings spread about three inches on either side. Pretty big tattoo for so tiny a woman, I thought, but everybody has their own taste. Wait...what is this? A row of surgical staples barely visible beneath the black ink of the butterfly tattoo's body! I grabbed the staple remover from my tray and carefully pulled each from her skin, revealing her small intestine. I probed gently with my fingers and felt something hard. On closer examination, I saw the meticulously sewn stiches in the membrane. I gently cut each thread with my scalpel and was shocked to discover a small plastic canister about two inches long. What on earth? Was Consuela a drug mule? I had heard of this method of smuggling drugs into the country but never seen it myself. I would need to examine the contents to know for sure, but nonetheless, she was carrying some sort of contraband, and I didn't imagine her to be the mastermind behind it.

The canister weighed three ounces on my scale, and I could feel liquid moving inside. I slowly removed the cap, withdrew a small sample in a dropper, and put it in the mass spectrometer for analysis and powered her up. While returning the cap to the canister, I noticed a tiny seam in the bottom. I pried on it with my fingernail, and it popped open, revealing a tiny onyx-colored bead. There was a pinprick of light blinking steadily from within it. What is this? I had never seen anything like it before. This case was suddenly becoming bigger than I ever imagined. I took the bead and sealed it in a tiny evidence bag and got a second bag for the canister just as the mass spec sounded its results.

The screen read 100 percent pure heroin! I grabbed the phone and called Bodie, bagged all the evidence, secured Consuela in the vault, and headed to the sheriff's office.

*****

Talib parked behind a monument in the cemetery and watched as Jess sped out of the driveway. He pulled slowly out and followed. When she arrived at the sheriff's office, he turned into the alley with headlights out and dialed Hassan. "They have the heroin. Probably put it in a safe for the night. What do you want me to do?"

Hassan replied, "Wait until the sheriff is alone and retrieve it. Leave no evidence of yourself!"

"Should I kill him?" asked Talib.

"No," replied Hassan. "Use the serum and put him to sleep. He will be too sick to remember anything when he wakes up, and it buys us some time. We don't want the American law enforcement after us for murder. Make it clean, and make it quick. I expect to see you here by sunrise. That is all."

CHAPTER SIX

When I walked into Bodie's office, the look on my face must have scared him.

"What did you find, Jess?" He sat stone-faced while I began.

"I found a pendant with the victim's name engraved on it. Consuela, she is South American. We will need to run her photo through AFIS to see if there are any warrants or missing persons' reports.

"It appears she is a drug mule. I found this canister surgically implanted in her small intestine. It is 100 percent pure heroin concentrate weighing three ounces. I have no idea what the street value of this is."

"I will need to notify the FBI of this, and since the victim is not from this country, I think the whole alphabet will be involved! CIA, FBI, ATF, CSP, DEA. Wow. This is big, Jess!" said Bodie.

"That is only part of it, Bodie," I said. "Look." I handed him the small plastic bag with the bead in it. He stared at the blinking red light.

"What the hell? Is this a tracking device?"

"I think so. I have never seen anything like it, but something is transmitting. If so, that means whoever owns this heroin knows where it is!"

Bodie took a deep breath and exhaled with a loud *whew!* "How did she get into Echo Creek?"

"I think I have the answer to that. I found a large amount of gray silt in her bra lining, and it looks like her swim may have started in the Dolores River. We need to get the rangers' reports on commercial rafting trips and boat launches in the last few days. Maybe we can find her boat. I doubt she walked in. It's a theory but worth investigating."

Bodie replied as he looked at his watch, "Right. Good thought. Jeez, it is almost 2:00 a.m. You should go home and get some rest. I will make some calls and get the feds on this. We can regroup in the morning. And, Jess, Good work!"

"Thanks, Bodie, you get some rest too. See you in the morning."

*****

As Jess walked out the front door to her van and drove away, Talib slipped in the front door of the sheriff's office and waited patiently for the right moment to strike. Bodie was sitting at his computer with the canister on the desk in front of him. He was reading furiously about heroin concentrate. It read: "When added to simple over-the-counter products such as powdered milk, it produces up to a kilogram of usable drug at a street value of over half a million dollars!" *No wonder these dealers want to follow their product*, he thought. *Wait until Jess hears this!* He picked up the canister and began to rise from his chair.

Talib struck at that moment from behind. The needle pierced Bodie's carotid artery, and the drug inside the syringe stole his feet as he collapsed on the floor. "Sleep, dog!" Talib hissed. He grabbed the canister with a sinister laugh and slid out the front door. Jumping into his car, he crept out of the alley, lights out, and headed down the street.

CHAPTER SEVEN

Shorty McDaniel stepped out the back door of his bar and locked the door. It had been a pretty slow night at the bar, and he was tired and ready to forget about it. As he opened the door to his old pickup, he saw a black sedan without lights on turn out of the alley behind the sheriff's office. He watched as it got to the corner, hit the lights, and sped away. He couldn't see more than one person in the car. Though unable to see a plate number, he did note it was not a Colorado plate. Was it white or light blue?

Seeing the lights still on at the sheriff's office, he decided to stop in and tell Bodie what he had just seen, thinking it was awfully late for Bodie to still be there.

Shorty was a big man, about six feet, eight inches tall, 290 pounds, long hair tied in a ponytail, and a handlebar mustache that was coiffed and refined. You don't mess with Shorty at the bar, that was for sure, but his good nature and hilarious sense of humor made him a local favorite of everyone. He often served as a volunteer with the sheriff's posse and welcomed the opportunity to dish out some mystery. He walked across the street and opened the front door of the sheriff's office.

He bellowed, "Don't shoot, it's just me!" and laughed. Hearing no response, he spoke. "Anybody home? Bodie?"

Shorty walked through the office door and saw Bodie crumpled on the floor. *What the?* "Bodie, Bodie!" He ran over to the body on the floor and could see that Bodie was breathing. Quickly dialing 911, Shorty spoke to the operator, "Get here quick! He's breathing, but he ain't waking up."

The operator instructed Shorty to stay with Bodie until the ambulance arrived and that it would be at least fifteen minutes. Shorty agreed and hung up the phone. He reached down and picked up his friend's wrist to take his pulse. A small plastic bag fell from Bodie's hand to the floor. Shorty picked it up and saw a black bead with a light blinking inside it. He stared wide-eyed at the object, looked at his friend lying on the floor scarcely breathing, and quickly opened the top drawer and shoved the bag inside and dialed Ben Doogan.

CHAPTER EIGHT

The coyotes were howling shrilly in the distance as I finally crawled into bed. God, I would be glad when they moved up to higher ground. I closed my eyes and tried to push the day's events out of my head.

In my dream, I could see Consuela's butterfly tattoo, and the wings began to flutter uncontrollably, as a buzzing noise pierced my ears. Like a shot, I sat straight up in bed with a gasp. My phone was ringing. It was Dad's ringtone. I grabbed for the phone on my nightstand, knocking it to the floor. As I stumbled out of bed, I picked up the phone. "Dad? Are you all right? Where are you?"

"Jess," he said, "you need to come to the station right now, something has happened. They took Bodie by ambulance to Cortez, don't know what happened yet. Shorty is here with me, I am acting sheriff. I need to know everything you found in your autopsy. Something bad is happening here, and we need to get to the bottom of it."

"I'll be right there."

CHAPTER NINE

When I arrived at the station, I could see Dad through the window, sitting at the computer and looking at Bodie's recent correspondences. It appeared that the FBI had been contacted, and they were sending an agent immediately, his arrival anticipated by 8:00 a.m. He looked at his watch, 4:15 a.m. That would give him some time to get details from Jess.

I entered the office and sat down. Shorty looked shaken but wide awake. He quickly told me what he had seen in the alley and described the scene in the office when he had entered. "I saw Bodie lying there on the floor, and it looked like he had just fallen over. Don't know if it was a heart attack or what. Then I called the ambulance and your pop. He had this here baggie in his hand," he said, handing me the evidence bag from the drawer. "Don't know what it is, but he had a death grip on it, that is for sure." I looked at the onyx bead steadily blinking in the bag.

Ben spoke, "What is this, Jess, and is there more evidence? I checked the safe and only found your photos and notes, and they indicated a canister? No sign of that anywhere here."

I swallowed deeply and said, "The canister was in its own bag, it contained three ounces of 100 percent pure heroin. That bead is a tracking device for the drug lord to follow his product. It looks like they did, and that car Shorty saw in the alley was probably carrying the person who took out Bodie. We need to find out from the hospital what happened. He was probably drugged, and the thief didn't realize we had removed the tracker from the canister and just ran off with the heroin."

Ben got on the phone immediately and called the hospital. The doctor on call responded, and we listened together on speakerphone as he described the small needle puncture in Bodie's neck and the results of the toxicology screen—

a high dose of flunitrazepam mixed with arsenic.

"It could have killed him, but the dosage was just low enough to knock him out and make him real sick," stated the doctor. "We have him on IV fluids and are monitoring his vital signs. Everything looks good, but it will be a few days before he is up to any visitors, and he probably won't remember any of this."

We sat quietly for a moment, taking it all in. Ben broke the silence. "The FBI has been notified, and there is an agent arriving here in about an hour. The e-mail noted that this heroin you found has been sourced from Las Vegas. The FBI has been investigating for months now, and your find in this poor girl's body is the best lead they have had. We also have the missing person's reports back, and there is a Consuela Rodriguez reported missing by her family in Colombia. The report said she and three of her friends, Maria Gonzales, Sophia Ramirez, and Marisol De Paulez were last seen at a nightclub together on April 12. All four of these girls are missing and presumed together. You only found Consuela, which means there could be more bodies out there. I will get the posse together, and we will continue a search up on the mountain."

Just then the front door opened, and FBI special agent Harlan Meeks entered the room.

CHAPTER TEN

Dressed in a tailored black suit, white shirt, bolo tie, cowboy boots, and a black Stetson, Harlan Meeks stood a strapping six feet tall with broad shoulders, ebony skin, cinnamon-brown eyes, and a row of white teeth that lit up the room.

My heart skipped a beat, and I instinctively touched my hair.

He introduced himself. "Harlan Meeks, Special Agent, FBI Las Vegas. You must be Bodie Martin," he said to Dad.

Ben shook his hand and replied, "No, sir, I am acting Sheriff Ben Doogan. This is my Deputy, Shorty McDaniel, and my daughter Jess Doogan, medical examiner."

"I see where she gets that red hair, pleasure to meet you."

Harlan smiled at me and said, "Jess, forgive me, but all this time I thought you were a guy. My apology."

"No offense," I said. "It happens a lot."

"Where is Sherriff Martin?" Harlan asked.

Ben spoke up. "There has been quite a bit going down here since you left on your flight this morning. I presume you have reviewed all the data we sent?"

"Yes," Harlan replied. "We are grateful for your discovery. This heroin-ring investigation has been going on for months, and this is the first real lead we have. Do you have the canister?"

I interjected, "That is the problem, sir."

"Call me Harlan," he said with a smile.

I continued. "The heroin was stolen last night by who we think is the drug dealer. He poisoned Bodie with a needle in the neck before taking off with the drugs. Bodie will be fine, but he is still in the hospital. Anyway, what he failed to realize, though, is that I had two evidence bags. One with the drugs and one with the tracking device." I handed the onyx chip to Harlan.

He carefully examined it and said, "This needs to be sent to Langley for analysis immediately. Our techs should be able to break the code, and that will tell us where this tracker is being tracked from!"

"There is more, Harlan," I said. "We believe that Consuela, the victim, was traveling with three other girls, and our missing-persons search has revealed names and photos of all four of these ladies. I think it is possible they are all being forced to carry heroin. I found evidence of the river in Consuela's bra and believe she and the other girls may all have been trying to escape by boat. Bodie and I were going to travel down to Cortez and check with the rafting companies, park rangers, and others to see if any launches were made. We had some terrible flash flooding from the spring runoff, and the commercial river runners were not allowed on the water for a few days. I think we may find some information that could help us find them."

Harlan replied, "That is a great idea. Let me go with you. In the meantime, Ben, if you could overnight this tracker to this address and get it out this morning, then that will get this rolling." Harlan handed Ben a note containing the address.

"Will do," said Ben.

I looked at Harlan and said, "I hope you brought some different shoes, you are going to need them."

CHAPTER ELEVEN

Talib pulled the sedan into the barn and got out. Hassan stood by his Cessna with arms folded. "You have it?" he asked.

"Yes, cousin," said Talib. "Everything went exactly as planned. The sheriff will remember nothing, and the heroin is all here." He grinned and tossed the canister to Hassan.

"Excellent!" hissed Hassan. He took his manicured fingernail and pried open the bottom. Empty! "You fool!" he growled. "The tracking device is missing! How could you be so stupid! If the FBI has it, they will be able to reverse track and find it all and us! Idiot! I should know better than to expect you would get this right! Give me the key, now!" he snarled.

Talib reached into his pocket for the lockbox key, and a look of terror washed over his face. He pulled both his pockets inside out. Empty! "Uh, uh," he stammered. "Hassan, it was there I swear. Kreschev gave it to me when we left. It was in my pocket, I swear!" His face paled, and with voice quivering, Talib choked out the truth. "The girl, Consuela, she must have taken it from me!"

"So your selfish desire for this woman's mouth on your manhood led you to this? Maybe I should remove that manhood from you, cousin, and make you the impotent idiot you are!" yelled Hassan as he threw a vicious kick into Talib's groin.

"Maleek, bring me my tablet." Maleek reached into the cockpit of the plane and pulled out his tablet. There on the screen they could plainly see a cluster of three blinking lights along what appeared to be a river, and the fourth was nowhere to be found. "They must have sealed the package with lead. We have thirty-six hours at best before they are on to us. Take Maleek and go to this river." Talib walked briskly to the tablet and looked at the GPS coordinates. Hassan zoomed in on the screen, and the satellite view let them plainly see a capsized rubber raft hung on a rock on the east side of the river. Looking closer, he could see a narrow access road leading to the water's edge. "This is how you will get there, Talib. Leave the bodies, and just bring me the drugs. If you fail again, you know the consequence."

Talib nodded and said, "I will not let you down, cousin."

"Now go," said Hassan, "and be back here in twenty-four hours!"

Talib turned and left. Hassan turned and walked to the cargo van in the back of the barn. He opened the door and looked at the six young women who were bound and strapped into the seats. He called out to his courier, "Miguel, take the cargo to Ignacio as planned. I will notify Black Hawk of the shortage and instruct a quick removal and destruction of the trackers. Make haste!"

CHAPTER TWELVE

I pulled up to the Echo Motel to pick up Harlan. I had packed my rope, dry gear, some sandwiches, water, and my .30-06 Springfield rifle with ammo. I hoped to not have to use it, but if necessary, I could shoot. Growing up on a ranch with cattle and coyotes, it was just part of life, though I had never pointed it at another human being. We would drive to Dolores and meet with the river rangers. I hoped my findings on Consuela's body were correct and that our trip would find the three missing girls. Harlan stepped out of his room carrying his sat phone, GPS, and a backpack. "Let's roll!" he said.

*****

Talib and Maleek had driven the eighty-mile trip to Dolores over Lizard Head Pass, oblivious to the stunning beauty of the fourteen-thousand-foot snowcapped Mount Wilson, Wilson Peak, and Sunshine Peak. Their focus was entirely on finding the remote and rarely accessed back trail to the river. Talib had failed his cousin twice and knew his life would be over if he failed again. The coordinates were close, according to the GPS, and they scanned the forest for the tiny two-track that the GPS had revealed. After passing the mark three times, Maleek finally saw the downed tree covered in brush that lay across the trail's entrance. They removed the chainsaw from the truck bed and carefully cleared an opening. After driving through, they returned the brush to hide their trespass and slowly maneuvered the SUV down the rutted, debris-covered road. It was a good three miles of winding, twisting, bumping road when they finally saw the river.

"This is it," said Talib. "We will hide the truck. Cover it with brush just in case someone saw anything."

They picked up their packs, guns, and a sharp knife. Once the women were found and the drugs were removed, there would be no burial. "Feed them to the fish!" had been Hassan's words. It would be done.

CHAPTER THIRTEEN

Harlan and I arrived at the ranger station about 8:30 a.m. and saw a young man in uniform hooking up his fourteen-foot drift boat to his ranger truck. We exited our car and approached the vehicle, showed our credentials, and introduced ourselves. Daniel Sparks couldn't have been more than twenty-five years old and had the shining excitement and enthusiasm in his eyes that couldn't help but bring a smile to your face. He listened wide-eyed as we told him what we were doing there and asked if he knew of any launches the day before yesterday.

"We had to close the river to the public due to dangerous water levels," Daniel told us. "There was a commercial multiday trip scheduled to leave that morning with six boats and twenty-four people. They are rescheduled to launch tomorrow. We did get a report that one of their twelve-foot rafts that had been moored at the launch was missing. We just assumed it had broken from its tie and floated down the river empty. I am actually going out now to try to locate it and make sure the flooding hasn't changed the river dramatically from the maps. There are some class V rapids on this river that, at different water levels, can be very tricky. We like our guides to know what is coming."

"Well," I said, "we would like to ride with you on this trip. We believe that the missing raft was taken by four young women trying to escape the drug cartel. We have found one of the missing girl's bodies in Echo Creek."

Daniel's eye's widened. "There is a large rapid just above the tributary. It is possible they flipped, and she was swept away in the flood."

"Yes," I replied, "I agree. Some of the physical evidence I found on her body indicated she started her journey in this river. I want to see it and hopefully find clues to the other missing girls."

"What supplies to you carry in the dry box, Daniel?" asked Harlan.

"I pack a first aid kit, a .357 Magnum pistol for scarin' bears, knife, extra life jacket, water, a couple of MREs, shovel, ammo can, toilet paper, sat phone, and a toolbox."

Harlan handed him my .30-06, rope, our water containers, and phones. We jumped aboard Big Red and headed for the launch site.

*****

Talib and Maleek stood at the edge of the river, looking upstream, as the silty white water roared past them, racing down the riverbed deeper into the canyon. According to the pings from the drug canisters, they were at least two miles downstream from their stash.

"It looks like a fisherman's trail going up. We will follow this, and if we are fortunate, Maleek, you will not have to cross this river to get to the girls."

"But, Talib, I cannot swim," said Maleek.

"This is not my problem but yours," hissed Talib. "We cannot fail."

The two headed up the narrow trail, navigating over the rocks and up the side of a cliff. As they started down, the river was narrowing sharply, and the roar from the rapids up ahead was deafening.

CHAPTER FOURTEEN

We arrived at the Bradfield Bridge launch site on the Dolores and rigged the dory for the trip through Paradox Canyon. Daniel took the lead, giving us a standard safety talk on what to do in case of a flip, how to high-side the craft, and commands for passengers in a drift boat. Mostly we were to stay still and heed his calls to shift our positions in the boat, and we were happy to accept his expertise in this situation. Daniel secured the bowline, took the oars, and pulled into the current. The dory glided into the river like a swan, and we shot downstream in a graceful dance. "Our first rapid is about fifteen minutes away," he said. "Water is running at about 4,500 cubic feet per second, so we are cruising. Two days ago it was over seven thousand, and we had to close it. Some of these rapids wash out at high water levels, and others become Niagara Falls. The first rapid coming up is called Snoozer. At low water you don't even know it is there, but at this level we don't want to be asleep. There is a large rock on river left that causes a sharp turn in the river, and that creates a hole on river right that we don't want to hit. Just stay still, and we should be able to snake straight through on the tongue and be fine."

Harlan grinned at me. "Let's do this!"

Just as he described, Snoozer was upon us, and we shot through the slot like an arrow. "*Woo-hoo! Yes!*" shouted Daniel. His exuberance made us both laugh out loud.

"Nice job, Daniel!" said Harlan. "What is coming up next?"

He replied, "We have flat water for about a mile and then the Chutes."

"What are the Chutes?" I asked.

Daniel smiled and said, "It's our Dolores roller coaster. About a quarter-mile wave train on river right that runs tight against the cliff wall. At lower water levels, we let passengers swim this section, and it is always a highlight for them. Today, however, I suggest we all stay in the boat. The standing waves will be anywhere from four to eight feet high. I won't know until we get there, but get ready for a fun run for sure!"

Harlan smiled back and said, "There is no question you love your work, Daniel, and you are an excellent boatman and guide. Maybe we can do this again sometime when the stakes aren't so high. Right now, we need to find the spot where Consuela was caught in the flood, and I think that from there, our other three victims will be close by."

"You are right," said Daniel. "After the rapid, the river widens and slows with hard currents pushing right…just below there is where Echo Creek diverts. There is an eddy called 'Keeper' on the right, and if any boats get caught in there, it takes brute strength or assistance from another boat to break the eddy line and get back into the current. It is possible they flipped the raft in the Chutes and were swept downstream. My guess is the boat will be in Keeper."

"Let's find out!" I said.

Daniel pointed the bow at the wave train, and we slid into the rapid. The first wave lifted the bow straight up in the air, and I lost my balance, falling backward into Harlan. He grabbed me and yelled, "Hang on, I've got you!" I marveled at the power in his grip. Daniel continued to steer the dory through the next wave, which dropped us forward with equal velocity. Harlan fell forward, and we both lay on the floor soaked from the wave and the standing water in the boat.

"Bail!" yelled Daniel. Harlan grabbed the bucket and began furiously tossing out buckets of water as we hit the final wave. I watched the muscles in his arms ripple and the veins in his neck distend with each exertion. The sun shining on his ebony skin reminded me of a black stallion posturing for his mares. *God, he is so handsome! I haven't had thoughts or feelings like this in years!*

The Chutes ended abruptly, and the river smoothed and continued on her path. Gathering my composure, I congratulated Daniel on an excellent run and settled back into my seat in the stern.

*****

Talib stepped out from the wooded trail onto the sandy beach on river left. It was a popular lunch spot for the commercial rafting trips, with spectacular views of the canyon walls and winding river. Upstream, about two hundred yards or so, he could see something blue across the river, bobbing and seemingly stuck in a wide circular motion of water. A large boulder blocked his view of the bow of this boat, but he was certain it was a raft and that his heroin was there. The tracking lights showed a cluster of three right at the spot. If the girls were behind those rocks on land, he wouldn't know without crossing the river. He looked downstream for a shallow place to cross and at the vicious rock climb it would take to get back upstream to the raft. Maleek groaned in protest at the prospect in front of them, but Talib's icy black stare scared him more than drowning. As they headed down the beach to cross, Talib thought he heard the sound of voices coming from above them. *There is someone coming! Hide!*

CHAPTER FIFTEEN

We continued down the river, watching the shoreline for any signs of the other girls. Daniel was standing on the oars, reading the water as it twisted and swirled. "There up ahead about three hundred yards river right, that's Keeper. I see the raft," he said. Harlan grabbed his binoculars and honed in on the spot. He could plainly see the bottom of the blue NRS twelve-foot raft as it bobbed and bounced in the eddy.

He handed me the binoculars, saying, "It looks like the bowline is stuck in between a crack in the boulders."

"That is what is holding it in place," Daniel interrupted. "If we go in there, we will play hell getting out, especially trying to tow out that raft. The river is moving too fast for me to get behind the boulder it is stuck on. We will have to go by and climb back over to it on the rocks."

I looked at the rock cliff and shook my head no. "Daniel, is there an eddy on river left we can stop in? I need to think." He looked ahead and artfully drove the bow across a small eddy line. We scraped the rock wall, and the stern sucked down, filling the floor with water before righting itself. We bailed the boat and sat quietly for a moment.

Harlan broke the silence. "I think Daniel is right here, Jess. Look how fast that current is going by. I don't think we should get stuck over there."

I said, "Well, we have only one chance at this, but it will be worth it if it works." I reached into the dry box and pulled out my rope. "Dad and I team roped for years, I was header, he was heeler. If

38

I can get a rope around that boulder when we float by, we can pull in behind it and tie on. Can you ferry this boat across the river and get upstream of that boulder? That should slow us down enough for me to make the throw."

Daniel replied, "I can give it my best shot, ma'am."

"Call me Jess. Let's do it then," I said. We nosed back into the current, and I took my place standing in the stern. Daniel angled the bow across the river and began pulling hard on the oars. We were getting closer: thirty yards, twenty, fifteen. I whirled the rope around my head and released, and the loop sailed through the air and landed perfectly over the top of the boulder. Harlan grabbed me by the waist while the bow swung back downstream. As the rope jerked tight, we both pulled back as the dory slid to a stop against the cliff wall. He secured the rope through the bow carabiner and pulled us up snug.

"Yee ha!" shouted Daniel. "Now that was something!"

We all enjoyed the levity of the moment before changing gears to the dangerous task ahead.

*****

Talib and Maleek watched from the cliff across the river. "It seems our work will be done for us," Talib said. "They will likely pull off the river where we walked in. There is cell signal there, flat ground, and a way out to the highway. We will be waiting for them. Be sure both clips are full for your weapon. These people won't know what hit them. Maleek smirked. Let the fun begin." They turned and headed back to the beach.

CHAPTER SIXTEEN

Harlan climbed out first onto the rock, found good footing, and reached out to pull me and Daniel up. We stood looking down the other side of the rock at the bottom of the raft, bouncing and banging into the cliff wall. Sure enough, the bowline was snagged tightly in a crack in the rock. We carefully lowered ourselves down for a closer look. There was something barely visible on the side of the raft just below the water's surface. Harlan gingerly crawled out onto the bottom of the raft and lay flat. He reached over the side for whatever it was we were seeing and gasped. "It is a foot!" he exclaimed. "Good lord, it is a woman's foot!" He took hold with both hands and from his knees exhumed the body from her watery grave, pulling her onto the raft bottom. Her ankle was bound tightly, and the remainder of the rope was taut. Harlan took his knife and freed her.

"It looks like Marisol!" I said. "She tied herself into the boat! How stupid! Oh my god! Feel around for the others, Harlan." He crawled forward and reached into the icy water again. Sure enough, a foot, a rope, a body of another young woman came into view. He pulled her in and cut the rope, and we identified Maria. Harlan reached into the water again and found our final victim, Sophia. The fourth rope tie floated loosely in the water, revealing the knotted loop that must have failed to hold Consuela. These poor women thought they would be safe by tying themselves in the boat. What a tragedy. Now we had to get them down the river. First it would require flipping the raft back over to right it.

Daniel and I braced ourselves against the rock wall, and Harlan carefully slid the dead girls' bodies over to the edge. We pulled them up onto the rocks one at a time and secured them. Next, Daniel went to the dory and got his throw rope. We would have to tie the line through the two side "D" rings to get leverage and try to use the eddy line to give us the extra push we needed. Harlan was still on the raft and rigged the line. Upon completion, he came up on the rocks with us. "First, we will need to cut the bowline and free the boat. Then I need all of us to pull on this rope when the raft finishes its circle. Are we clear?"

"Yes," Daniel and I replied. Harlan took his knife and sliced through the bowline. The raft pulled away from the rock and began to follow the eddy's swirl. As it reached the eddy line, we all pulled back as hard as we could, and the raft popped over and righted itself. We cheered! We snagged the raft back into the rock and gently returned the girls' bodies onto the floor of the righted rubber raft.

Daniel would take the lead on moving the bodies to shore. His plan was simple. He gave Harlan the spare oar from the dory to use as a lever to push off the rock face and get out of the eddy. Then he took the bowline from the raft and threaded it through the stern ring on the dory. "Now," he said, "when I pull out into the current, you push off the rock, and that should get you out behind me. The raft will go faster than my boat, so, Jess, you will need to pull the line through the ring and snub the nose to my stern. Got it?"

We confirmed, and Daniel took to the oars. His plan was perfect. The dory jerked the bowline of the raft, Harlan pushed off with the oar, and we were once again heading down the canyon. Daniel said, "There is a lunch spot up ahead on river left with a large beach. We can get out there and secure everything. Sometimes I can get cell service standing on the rocks above it, and we can get some help. There is river access from the highway here too."

"Sounds perfect," I said.

*****

Talib and Maleek watched as the dory and raft headed toward the beach. Perched high above in the rocks, they would have a clear shot at their quarry, short of just one tree that was used to tie off boats and probably afforded much-needed shade on a summer river trip. "Stay out of sight, Maleek, and wait for my signal. We will both need to fire at the same time. I doubt the ranger carries a weapon, but I am certain the FBI agent will be armed and dangerous."

CHAPTER SEVENTEEN

Daniel expertly pushed the bow of his boat through the current and guided it toward the beach. As it grew closer to land, I jumped to the shore and grabbed the bowline, pulling the boat onto the sand. The raft jackknifed behind the dory and came to a stop. I tied the boat to the tree as Harlan and Daniel lifted the bodies of the three dead girls out of the raft and carefully laid them out on the sand. The cold water had kept them almost lifelike in their preservation. It was obvious they had drowned, and I was hopeful that it had been quick and painless.

I looked up from my thoughts and saw Daniel leaning over a boulder on the river's shore, retching violently. The adrenaline had worn off, and reality sunk in.

Just as I was about to step forward and give him a hand, a shot rang out from above. It sounded like one gun, but a bullet hit the boulder and ricocheted out into the river. The second tore through Daniel's shoulder, sending him rolling and screaming to the ground. Harlan pulled his service weapon from his vest and began firing in the direction that the bullets had come from. I grabbed Daniel's legs and began pulling as hard as I could to drag him under cover of the tree. Shots continued to rain down on the sand. My .30-06 rifle was in the dry box on the dory, along with a first aid kit. We needed both desperately. Harlan handed me his backup gun and a full clip. "I want you to shoot straight up there at those rocks." He pointed to the position. "Shoot every round, reload, and shoot again. I want them holed up there, unable to shoot. That should give me time to get to the first aid kit and your rifle. On the count of three. One, two, three!"

I began firing wildly toward the rocks as Harlan burst out from under the tree and ran to the dory.

He reached into the box, got the first aid kit, rifle, and shells, and was back before I had finished half of the second clip. The moment I stopped firing, shots came flying back at us. "Good job," said Harlan. "I know where they are. I will go around back through the brush and come in behind them. I want you to continue to shoot and keep them distracted." He quickly looked at Daniel, who was bleeding heavily through his light jacket. Grabbing a tourniquet from the first aid kit, he tightened the wrap around Daniel's shoulder and back. "The shot is a through and through, you will be okay. Just lay still, we've got you." He turned and gave me a brilliant smile. "This will be like shooting fish in a bowl. Are you ready?"

I smiled weakly back at him and said, "Just be careful. We can't get through this without you."

"I love it when you get needy!" He winked at me and disappeared into the brush.

*****

Talib had switched positions up in the rocks and was now able to get a shot closer to the trees. He could see Daniel leaning up against the tree the dory was tied to. He shot toward him, but the bullet had no chance. The shot was way too high. "Maleek!" he yelled. "I am going down to finish this. Cover me." He headed around the rock boulders down the narrow trail just as Harlan came around the brush and headed up. Harlan pulled his Glock from his shoulder harness and fired, hitting Talib directly between the eyes and dropping him. He grabbed the body, dragged him down the trail, and stuffed him in the brush. Then he turned and headed back up the trail to find the second shooter. Maleek had heard the gunshot and was trying desperately to make his way down over the rocks and off the trail to escape. Harlan could hear the rocks and dirt falling up ahead. He rounded a corner and saw Maleek sliding down the side of the cliff.

Taking careful aim, he shot at his legs. Maleek's left knee buckled as the bullet tore through the lateral ligaments and blood poured out like rain. The screams of pain were deafening.

Harlan made his way over to Maleek and grabbed him by the arms, pulling him up the side of the rocks onto the trail leading down to the beach. "Get the zip ties out of the boat and cuff this creep." Harlan's anger was alive on his face, and the tone of his voice made me leap into action. We secured Maleek's hands, slowed the bleeding in his leg, and for the first time in hours, took a deep breath and stopped moving.

"We will need to get a helicopter in here," I said.

"Yes," agreed Harlan.

Daniel spoke weakly. "If you go back up the trail toward the road about a quarter mile, we have been able to get cell service from there."

"On it," Harlan replied. "Keep a gun on this guy, though I doubt he will give you any trouble." Maleek had passed out from the pain. "I will be back shortly."

CHAPTER EIGHTEEN

Harlan tore through the overgrown trails with the grace and speed of a bull elk, finally reaching an open area in the trees that, at last, had strong-enough signal to make his call. His first was to emergency dispatch where he ordered a medevac helicopter, explaining that there were two gunshot victims needing assistance. One was a prisoner requiring a guard and the second a forest ranger with nonlife-threatening injuries. He then proceeded to request a ground ambulance to carry four dead bodies to the morgue. He and Jess would need transportation as well. The dispatcher on the line responded with disbelief at the volume of this emergency but did his job as ordered. Harlan hung up his phone and dialed again, this time to FBI headquarters in Las Vegas.

He reported the entire incident and events to his superior, Agent Geoffrey Todd, who praised his work. "This could finally close this case for us, Harlan. We did get the results from Langley on the tracker. Our reverse-signal catch has the devices being tracked from a remote location in the Grand Mesa of Colorado not far from where you are. Our satellites have been searching the area, but there are too many trees to get a confirmation of any buildings, airstrips, or other hard proof of activity. I will need you to go and check it out yourself."

Harlan replied, "I will do that, sir, but first I would like the chance to question my prisoner. He may spill his guts. The guy is a total loser and, from what I see, a few crayons short of a box! I shot him in the knee, and he is in serious pain, but I think I can turn that into exactly what we want to know."

"Do what you need to do, Harlan," said Geoffrey. "I will send a couple of agents to Cortez to join you, and let's finish this!"

"Yes, sir," Harlan replied. "I want you to know we wouldn't be this far without the help of the Echo medical examiner, Jess Doogan. She has great instincts and amazing skills. I would like permission to bring her with me and finish what we started."

"Permission granted."

CHAPTER NINETEEN

The next couple of hours were a cluster of activity. The Life Flight helicopter landed, and the flight nurse and a police officer loaded the aircraft with the wounded men. Daniel was pale and dehydrated, but the fear was gone from his face, and the sparkle of adventure was twinkling in his pain-filled eyes. Maleek was unconscious from the excruciating pain in his knee and a bump on the head Harlan accidently administered with the butt of his Glock on the way to the landing sight. Harlan gave instructions to the officer to take both men to the hospital and have a twenty-four-hour armed guard on Maleek. FBI agents were coming to relieve the armed guard and should be there by day's end. The officer nodded and told Harlan the ambulance was en route and should arrive momentarily.

"Clear the area for takeoff, and we will see you at the hospital!" yelled the helicopter pilot.

We both stepped back and watched as the Airbus 155 twin-engine helicopter rose straight up and shot to the south. It was always amazing to see these birds fly, and we both stared admirably as the helicopter disappeared from view.

"Well, Ms. Doogan," said Harlan, "this has been quite a day. You did great work for us, and I would be honored if you would stay with this case to fruition."

"Can I do that? I am not FBI."

"No, you aren't, but you are skilled, smart, and intuitive. We never would have gone down this river without your insight. I want you to come to Las Vegas with me and finish this. First, we have to check out a break in the case on finding the leader here in Colorado. If you would join me for dinner tonight, I will fill you in on the details."

CHAPTER TWENTY

The ambulance arrived about fifteen minutes after the helicopter had left. The EMT helped us load the four dead bodies into the vehicle. Harlan instructed him to deliver the bodies to the hospital morgue, and there would be an FBI agent waiting to take custody. The young man nodded. He said, "When I was driving in here, I saw a truck in the woods covered in brush as though someone were trying to hide it. It may belong to one of these victims."

I said, "Take us there on your way out and wait. If the keys are still in it, we can drive it back to Cortez and admit it into evidence." The ambulance driver took us to the area and stopped. Harlan and I walked over to the hidden truck, removed the brush cover, and looked inside. Sure enough, the keys were in the ignition. Harlan opened the passenger door and the glove box. Inside was a cell phone. "Perfect!" he said. "We now have contact. Let's get to town now." We waved the ambulance driver off and watched him head down the rutted road. We started the truck and followed. The contact info on the cell phone could lead us to the mastermind of this horrific drug ring, and we were both anxious to get to the resources we would have with the FBI's mobile-command unit waiting in Cortez.

CHAPTER TWENTY-ONE

A couple of hours later, we arrived at the hospital. Daniel had been taken into surgery and was expected to recover fully. Maleek was not so fortunate. Harlan's shot in the knee completely destroyed the joint, and it would require replacement surgery for Maleek to ever bear weight on that leg again. In the meantime, the doctors treated the pain and waited for instructions from us. Harlan excused the doctors for the moment and shut the door behind them as they left. Turning to Maleek, he reached over and squeezed his leg. Maleek shrieked in pain.

"Who are you working for?" said Harlan calmly, with ice in his voice. Maleek groaned. "Answer me or I'll do it again, only this time I won't let go."

"Hassan Ramadi," Maleek whispered.

"What?" Harlan said.

"Hassan Ramadi. He is waiting for us now."

"Where?" shouted Harlan, pushing his finger deep into Maleek's knee.

Maleek screamed, "At the warehouse on the mesa! He has an airplane and will leave immediately if he doesn't hear from me before 5:00 p.m. today."

I looked at my watch, 3:30 p.m. "We have time."

Harlan handed Maleek the cell phone. "Call Hassan, tell him everything went as planned, and you will meet as ordered—put it on speaker." With the 9 mm gun barrel pressed on his temple, Maleek shakily dialed the phone.

Hassan picked up immediately and snarled, "Where are you?"

"We are in Cortez now. Everything went smoothly. We will be there by first light tomorrow morning," said Maleek.

"Good!" said Hassan. "Let me speak to Talib."

Harlan pressed the gun barrel deeper into Maleek's temple.

"Ah, sorry, sir, he is getting gasoline for the truck. Should I have him call you back, sir?"

"No, it's fine. I will see you soon. Good work."

The phone line went dead. Harlan removed the barrel of the gun from Maleek's temple, and we breathed a collective sigh of relief. "Now," said Harlan, "where is this mesa and airplane hangar?"

*****

Hassan hung up the phone and quickly dialed his backup man in Cortez. Miquel Juarez answered immediately. "Something is wrong. Find Talib. Maleek said they were at a gas station. I don't believe him. The tracking signals are off. I believe they have been captured. Check the police station, the hospital, impound lots, and government buildings. You understand? Find them and kill them before the FBI can get any information, then meet me in Las Vegas at Caesars." He hung up without waiting for a response.

*****

Harlan and I left the hospital armed with the location and insight on Hassan that we needed. We would head out in the morning and make our move. Harlan asked me to join him for dinner as he dropped me off at my motel room. "I saw an interesting-looking Italian place," he said, "when we drove through town. How about some pasta and a nice Chianti? I'm buying!"

"Are you asking me on a date, Meeks?"

"Guess I am." He grinned. "Can't think of anyone else I would rather break bread with."

CHAPTER TWENTY-TWO

Miguel Juarez drove slowly down Main Street, looking for Talib's truck. It was not to be found. He pulled his car into the parking lot at the hospital and drove slowly up and down each row. Still no sign of the truck. There was a black SUV with government plates parked by the emergency entrance, and a local police car had just pulled in. The officer exited his vehicle and went in the front entrance. *This must be the place.* He parked, entered the hospital, and went into the gift store. He purchased a set of scrubs and ducked into the restroom where he slipped them on and entered the facility.

In no time at all, Miguel found Maleek's room. It was obvious by the police guard sitting at a small table outside the door. This could be a problem. He would need a distraction. The syringe he carried in his pocket was filled with a euthanasia drug stolen from a veterinary clinic. He was to inject it into Maleek's IV bag and leave. It would take only seconds for the drug to stop the heart and was a foolproof plan short of the officer at the door. There was a restroom two doors down from Maleek's room that would be perfect for starting a small fire in the garbage. When the officer saw the smoke, he would run to try to put it out. Miguel could then execute his plan.

He walked casually down the hall toward the bathroom. The officer looked up and nodded.

Sliding quickly into the room, he lit a ball of paper towel on fire and stuffed it deep into the trash can. Smoke billowed slowly out. He left the restroom and walked past the officer and down to the end of the hall to wait. Five minutes had passed when the smoke alarm sounded. Smoke billowed out from under the bathroom door.

As expected, the officer leaped to his feet and ran into the bathroom. Miguel raced down the hall and into Maleek's room. He jabbed the needle into the bag, emptied the contents of the syringe, and sped out the door—down the hall and out of the hospital. Job done!

CHAPTER TWENTY-THREE

I stood in the shower and let the hot water massage my sore muscles. My arms and neck were covered in scratches from the underbrush, and there was a huge bruise on my butt from falling in the boat. Hope they have cushioned seats at the restaurant. I shampooed my hair and watched the mud and my stress disappear down the drain with the sweet smell of coconut.

Today I had watched a man die a violent death. Seen an innocent young man shot and terrified. Watched another have his knee blown off and carried three dead women packed with drugs out of the river. That was enough for one day. Dinner would be a civilized and welcome respite to this horrific day, and Harlan Meeks was someone I really wanted to get to know. I put on a clean pair of jeans and my light-blue blouse, wishing I had something a little sexier to wear. When I opened my door, I found Harlan poised to knock.

"You clean up good," he said, with that beautiful white smile. He was wearing all black as usual but had shaved the stubble off his face and smelled expensively delicious. "Shall we go?" He took my arm and escorted me to the car, held the door, and tucked me safely in. I felt my face flush and quickly pushed my thoughts back to the case.

We pulled up to the Trattoria Di Bernardone restaurant and went inside. I had never eaten there before but had heard good things, and frankly, I was starving! The aroma of garlic and basil filled my nostrils, and my stomach growled in anticipation.

The hostess took us to an intimate table in the corner under a Tiffany light where a bottle of Rocca De Frassinello and two glasses were poised and ready to serve. Harlan pulled out my chair and guided me into it with his palm on my back. The waiter uncorked the wine, poured a taste in the glass, and handed it to Harlan for his approval. "Eccellente!" exclaimed Harlan. The waiter then filled our glasses, bowed, and left us to explore the menu.

"Pretty fancy digs for this little town," he said and chuckled.

I replied, "Hey, we have culture in Colorado. Don't think you city boys know everything!" We laughed, touched glasses, and enjoyed the warm buzz, aroma, and each other's company. I ordered the veal parmigiana with a Caesar salad while Harlan chose the Fettuccini Alfredo with scallops.

"So, Harlan Meeks, what is your story? What made you become an FBI agent?

"Hey, I was going to do the probing here!"

"Ladies first," I said, batting my eyes and grinning like a teenage girl!

He chuckled softly and began, "Let's see, I grew up in Austin, Texas, was in ROTC throughout high school, and when I graduated from high school, I enlisted in the Air Force. I always wanted to fly fighter jets. I did my basic at Joint Base San Antonio Lackland in Texas, and once finished they moved me into the Helicopter Pilot Program and had me flying U60 Black Hawks. Not a fighter jet, but man are they amazing machines. I did two tours in Afghanistan and Iraq, fought the bad guys and investigated combat operations, which got me interested in solving crimes and finding answers. When my final tour was up, I left the military and applied to Quantico for FBI training. The rest is history!" He grinned. "Now your turn!"

At that moment, our meals arrived. "I am afraid you'll have to wait. I am starving." We both dived in with exuberance.

About five minutes into the feast, there was a collective reaction in the restaurant. Three armed police officers had entered and were talking to the hostess. A moment later she led them to our table. "Agent Meeks, Ms. Doogan, we need you at the station immediately. We will explain there." Harlan paid the restaurant bill, and we followed the officers out the door. Dinner would have to wait!

CHAPTER TWENTY-FOUR

The police chief and coroner were both at the station waiting for us. "There was an incident at the hospital," said the chief. "A fire was started in a bathroom, and our prisoner was poisoned. We think the fire was a deliberate distraction, and the deputy guarding the prisoner was pulled away from his post by the smoke coming out from under the bathroom door. No one saw anything unusual."

"I can't believe this!" shouted Harlan. "We had him! We know where he was going and now this! We are in the middle of nowhere where everybody knows everyone, and a complete stranger is able to infiltrate a secure zone and eliminate the most important discovery and information witness we have had in three years in an ongoing investigation for the biggest drug and prostitution ring in Las Vegas! Is that what you are telling me just happened? Is it? Is it?"

"Harlan, calm down," I said. "No one let this happen on purpose. C'mon! Take a deep breath. We know Maleek was to go to the Grand Mesa somewhere. Sooooo...let's go see what is there and then plan our next move."

Harlan's face was red, if black could be red, and his eyes pierced mine with a fire as hot as the one in the hospital bathroom. "I am sending Ross and his crew to the mesa. We are going to Las Vegas. There is no doubt in my mind that Hassan has left Colorado, and they are making plans to evade us once again. Get some things together. We are going to Vegas, and we are going to end this!"

CHAPTER TWENTY-FIVE

I drove the two hours back to Echo and stopped to update Dad on the events of the day. He was still acting as sheriff, but Bodie was scheduled to come back on duty in a couple of days. The town was still abuzz over all the shocking activities that had taken place. Shorty's bar was packed at midnight when I drove by and headed to my cabin to pack some clothes. Harlan had stayed in Cortez and would wait for me to return tomorrow. The FBI jet would fly us out midafternoon.

I pulled up to the cabin and got out of the car. Everything looked the same as I had left it. I unlocked the front door and entered the room, set down my bag, and turned on the TV. The *Late Late Show* was on, and some band I had never heard of was ripping a heavy-metal scream fest. I laughed out loud as I heard my mother's voice in my head yelling, "TURN THAT NOISE OFF! What is this world coming to? When I was a kid, music was musical, lyrics had meaning. It's no wonder you kids are all going wild." I quickly changed the channel. *Casablanca* was on. "Here's lookin' at you, kid." I went to my closet and perused through the elegant selections of jeans, lab coats, fleece pullovers, and there it was! My one little black dress. I would need that to pull off our cover in Vegas. I packed my essentials—cosmetics and some jewelry. That should do. Exhausted, I turned off the TV, rolled into my bed, and closed my eyes. The coyotes were howling in the distance as I drifted off to sleep.

CHAPTER TWENTY-SIX

Ben was at my door by 8:00 a.m. He would drive me back to Cortez to meet Harlan and fly out to Vegas. It would be a good opportunity to catch him up on some of the details left out in my earlier condensed version of the events. He listened intently as I described the shoot-out on the river, the conversation with Maleek, and what the bigger picture of this insidious drug ring was. "I know you know what you are getting into here, Jess," he said, "but don't you think the FBI could use one of their own female agents to go undercover with Meeks?"

"Sure they could," I replied. "But, Dad, this has been the most exciting case I have ever worked, and the FBI really likes my performance. They want to keep me on! I have to see this through."

"Well, you always were a stubborn little girl. Should be no reason you wouldn't be a stubborn grown-up lady! Just be careful, Jess. No case is worth dying for, and we—I—need you here. You know I love you, kid?"

"I know, Dad. I love you too. Everything will be just fine."

For the next hour, we drove in silence and finally arrived at the airport where the jet and Harlan stood waiting. I grabbed my suitcase, hugged Ben and Harlan, and boarded the plane.

CHAPTER TWENTY-SEVEN

From his twenty-ninth floor suite overlooking the gaming activities at Caesars Palace, Hassan watched carefully as his harem of hookers manipulated the room. The ladies went for as much as one thousand dollars an hour depending on the client, and each girl had an executive pimp, as it were, that determined her price. It was a beautifully designed and executed plan, and the volume of money generated each night was in the tens of thousands of dollars. Little of this cash went to the women, however. Hassan had abducted these girls from many South American countries and threatened their families if his demands weren't met. He used the money they earned to smuggle in the raw heroin from Afghanistan and to finance his labs to process the powder. These labs were strategically located in California, Colorado, and Washington. Hassan was the godfather of the western territory, and no other cartels dared step on his empire. He knew the FBI was watching, and after the debacle in Colorado he was anxious to get in front of the problem and move on.

CHAPTER TWENTY-EIGHT

Our jet began the descent into Sin City. Even in the full light of day, the neon strip sparkled like fireworks below. Fortunes were made and lost by the second in this place, and if you wanted to be invisible, there was no better place to hide. We were about to ferret out an invisible monster, and I could feel the excitement and anticipation. When we landed, there were three black SUVs with FBI agents waiting for us, and we were ushered into the front vehicle with Agent Todd.

"Harlan, Ms. Doogan, welcome to Gomorrah," said Geoffrey. I will get right to it."

"It appears that a private jet landed late last night registered to a Dr. Vladimir Kreschev. Airport security said the pilot looked Middle Eastern, and his flight plan showed an origination from Grand Junction, Colorado. We contacted the airport there, and they showed no such flight. We believe the pilot of this jet falsified these records. We have video surveillance from the airport, and this is a photo of the man we believe to be Hassan Ramadi. He is from the Sunni tribe in Iraq and runs a dry cleaning business next to Caesars Palace. The dry cleaning is legitimate, but our detectives have observed him as residing in the hotel on the twenty-ninth floor. We think this is where he runs his prostitution ring. Your discovery, Ms. Doogan, of the butterfly tattoos on the girls really brought this home for us. Hassan's harems are all tattooed with this. Here is a photo of one of the girls working the room."

We looked closely at the beautiful young woman who was scantily covered with her midriff exposed. You could plainly see the butterfly tattoo on her navel accentuated with an emerald-colored jewel. Probably to hide the numerous incisions. Geoffrey continued, "We want you two to pose as a couple looking for a three-way." I gasped. "Don't worry, we will have eyes on you all the time. When you get a hit, take the girl to your room, and we will be watching. She should be able to give us the information we need to follow the money. That should get us to Hassan. Are we clear?"

Harlan smiled at me reassuringly. "Perfectly, sir. I will need a tux, and let's get Jess here into something red and hot!"

I groaned.

*****

Harlan looked fabulous as we entered the hotel lobby to check in. I didn't look too bad myself, considering I hadn't worn a backless dress, let alone a dress in years! My long red hair was pulled up and pinned with an elegant jeweled peacock feather. The feather housed a tiny microphone and video camera that gave the guys in the mobile unit full access to everything we saw and heard. We checked in and had the concierge take our bags to the room, and then we headed to the casino lounge.

The slot machines played a symphony of bells, buzzers, clanks, and whistles as eager gamblers waged their pocket change and life savings in the hopes of hitting the jackpot. Blackjack tables were filled, and billows of smoke disappeared into the giant filter systems at an equal rate to the pure oxygen pouring back out. We wandered casually among the tables, continually scanning the crowd for any of Hassan's harem. I spotted her first. "There, up at the bar hitting on that old man in the purple jacket," I said.

Harlan replied, "Easy mark in that coat, the guy has more money than taste!" He laughed. "Let's go grab us a cocktail."

We eased up to the bar, and Harlan ordered a couple of dirty martinis, with two olives, and flashed his brilliant smile at the young woman, giving her a wink. We then headed over to the craps table and bought some dice. Harlan threw a seven and won his first bet.

Placing a second, he won again then again. A small crowd gathered as he continued to win toss after toss.

Included in that crowd was our young hooker. She completely ignored me as she sidled up to Harlan, letting her large breasts brush his arm. "Buy you a drink?" she asked.

He said, "Tequila Sunrise."

She answered smoothly and seductively, "Do you want to see the sunrise with me?"

"I am here with my wife," he answered, and she glanced over at me, brown eyes flashing approvingly.

"I like American women, especially with the red hair. They are energetic in bed. One thousand dollars for a three-way, five thousand dollars all night. What do you think, mister…?"

"Smith," he replied. "Bob Smith. This is my wife, Carol."

"Well, Mr. and Mrs. Smith, shall we play?"

"What's your name, darlin'?"

"Alena," she said.

"Well, Ms. Alena"—Harlan threw the dice once more, rolling snake eyes—"let's do this."

*****

Alena asked for our room number, excused herself for a moment, and we watched as she whispered into a large and scary-looking man's ear. She nodded and walked seductively back to us. Taking both our arms, she guided us to the golden elevator doors, and we headed up to our room on the tenth floor at the end by the staircase. We approached our room, and I noticed there was a silver tray outside the door with a bottle of champagne on ice, three flutes, and a bowl of fresh strawberries. Alena winked at us both and said, "A gift from me. I like to get bubbly before we play." We thanked her, and Harlan slipped the key into the slot, and we entered the room.

The second the door closed behind us, three armed FBI agents swarmed around Alena and led her to the dining table. She looked terrified. I stepped in to calm her. "Alena, these people are all FBI agents and are here to help you. We know that a terrible man kidnapped you from your country and is using you for prostitution and to smuggle heroin. We have found four of your friends, and they are all dead. You will be next if we don't get to this man. We need your help."

"I can't go against Hassan, or he will kill my family!" she cried.

"That won't happen, Alena," Harlan said. "We are the FBI, and we have ways to catch these criminals. We will get you back to your family and all the other girls for that matter. You have to trust us."

"What do I need to do?" she asked.

CHAPTER TWENTY-NINE

Director Todd opened his briefcase and pulled out an earpiece. "Alena," he said, "we are going to put this device in your ear. Your hair will cover it, and you will be able to hear us talking to you. We can hear everything going on around you. You must remain natural and can't be nervous. Your boss is a hideous, evil man, and he will not think twice about making good on his promise to you if he finds out. All you have to do is take this money." He handed her three thousand dollars, which would cover three hours. "Deliver it to Hassan as you always do, and we will have agents staked out at the dry cleaners ready to make the bust. Now, what is your exact route?"

Alena explained that she would take the elevator to the parking garage and exit out the car ramp on foot. She then would walk the two-block length of the hotel and go into the dry cleaners.

"There is a large sign on the wall to your right when you first come in," she explained. "It is actually a door with a staircase that goes down to the office. Hassan's man will take my money, and then I go back out on the floor. Unless…"

"Unless what?" I asked.

"Unless it is my turn to carry the drugs. I never know when they will take me, but if they do, I am taken out the back to the alley and loaded in a van. I do not know where they take me as I am blind-folded. Then we get to the place I know only the inside."

"Describe that to us. But first, how long are you riding in the car?" asked Harlan.

"That's easy. I am paid by the hour and know the hour to the minute, or else I am to pay for the extra time. It was exactly one hour and nine minutes!"

"That's good, that's good!" I said. This would help us tremendously. "Get a map and look at areas approximately eighty miles from here in every direction." Agent Todd pulled up the satellite imagery on his computer and keyed in a code. A detailed overlay gave a perfect view of the strip. He then changed GPS coordinates, and the map quickly revealed the arteries leaving the Neon City of Sin. There was I15 that ran northeast to Mesquite, which was in range, and southward I95 went to Laughlin, which too could be an option. To the northwest was Carson City, but that seemed to be out of path we had been pursuing, and it was a good three hours to get there, so that left Laughlin or Mesquite. We all agreed that Mesquite was the likely target but would send a small contingency of agents into Laughlin for insurance. Harlan and I were on the Mesquite team.

"Now, Alena, describe to us what you can remember of the inside of this building," said Harlan.

"It was very noisy," Alena said thoughtfully. "I heard loud trucks and metal banging all the time. It smelled like a dumpster. There was no carpet. My shoes echoed when I walk. Then we went into a smaller room. It felt warmer and brighter under my hood. They gave me drugs to sleep...lay me on a table, and when I woke up the heroin was in me."

"Then what?" I asked.

"Then they put the hood back on my head, and I was taken to a van where they drove me to the drop. Sometimes it's in Seattle, I know because I hear them talking, and sometimes it is in Denver. I know this too because I heard the driver say after he dropped us that he was going to the Denver Western Stock Show and buy a pig from his daughter's 4-H club. I do not know what this 4-H is, but he sounded very proud. Oh yes, also, sometimes Hassan would fly us to someplace in Colorado. I do not know where, but he has an airstrip that he lands the plane on, and then we get into a van and end up in Denver."

"How long a ride is it from the airstrip to Denver?" asked Harlan.

"It takes three hours and ten minutes and feels like we are climbing many hills," said Alena.

"That airstrip has to be somewhere in Dolores County," I said. "It's the least populated area of the entire state. There are thousands of acres of land up there, both rugged terrain and flat mesas. Use the satellite and search San Miguel and Dolores County for any location open enough to land a plane. His place will be isolated for sure, so it won't likely be too close to any towns."

Alena sat quietly as we perused the satellite imagery on Todd's screen.

There seemed to be many landing strips across San Miguel County. Not surprising, as Telluride, the county seat, was home to many billionaires and celebrities who used those homes just a few times a year for a ski vacation in winter or a summer playground on the pristine rivers and lakes which abound in the San Juans. It would not be unreasonable that one or more might have a private airstrip to come and go as they pleased. Dolores County, on the other hand, was lightly populated and had much less wealth. It would be the perfect place to hide out and remain invisible.

"I think we should focus our search there."

"Great idea, Jess. I told you guys she was a ringer," said Harlan. "Let's take a look!

Geoffrey keyed in the coordinates, and the satellite zoomed in. We could see mountaintops, roads, rooftops, barns, and sheds but so far nothing that looked like a potential airstrip. He widened the search, and we all scoured the images. Just as we were about to give up, we saw a flash of light. "Look there! It is a metal building in the trees, there!" Todd said and pointed. He zoomed in tighter, and sure enough, a large metal building suitable as an airplane hangar was nestled in the trees with a wide-open field stretching at least half a mile outside its doors.

"That's it!" I said excitedly.

"Get the GPS coordinates and send a team up there, now!" said Harlan. We all cheered.

When the celebration ended, we turned to Alena. It had been about two hours since we entered the hotel room, and time was running out. We sewed a small tracking device into her dress while going over her instructions. Hopefully, Hassan was trafficking her to Denver. We would be going in tonight to make the bust if Alena didn't come out into the alley after her money drop. At two hours and fifty-five minutes, Alena opened the hotel-room door and slipped out into the hall and down the stairs.

*****

Two ATF agents were in place in the alley, waiting for any sign of activity. They were to take photos only and report details. The tracking device in Alena's dress would keep us apprised of her location. Harlan and I would be ready for the tail in one vehicle, while four other agents were ready in another. Tensions were high as we waited.

CHAPTER THIRTY

Alena entered the dry cleaners and slipped down the staircase behind the picture. A huge Russian man—hairless on top with eyebrows that stretched into a single line across his forehead, making him look like he was looking at her through a window—stood waiting. She walked timidly toward the man and handed him the three thousand dollars. He counted it slowly, pulled thirty dollars from the stack, and handed it back to her. That was her one percent cut she received for every John. It wasn't much, but for Alena, it was more than her father earned per week on his job in Brazil at the coffee-bean plantation. She secretly sent him and her mother at least one hundred dollars every month. If Hassan knew this, he would certainly kill her, but she didn't care. Her family was all she had, and all she wanted was to get back to them. Hopefully, she could count on us to make this happen, and we were in as much need of her intel as she of our rescue. Could be a win-win, or it could be a tragedy; that was yet to play out. Alena took her money and was about to leave when the Russian grabbed her by the arm, slipped a hood over her head, and snarled, "Your job is yet to be finished. You leave tonight!"

CHAPTER THIRTY-ONE

A van was parked with the engine running in the alley outside the dry cleaners. Two men were in the vehicle; both looked Hispanic. From the building across the alley, two ATF agents had guns pointed at the tires on the van, ready to fire if given the order. Two more FBI agents were hidden in the alley, watching carefully. An undercover LVPD officer was checking in a bag of cleaning to the receptionist inside the dry cleaners while watching for Alena to come out from the staircase. Harlan and I were sitting in his black Challenger, a block south of the van, watching quietly. The front and back were secured, so all we could do now was wait.

Fifteen minutes passed when the rear door of the dry cleaners opened, and the big Russian led the hooded Alena, now dressed in jeans and a sweater, out to the van and helped her into the back seat. ATF agent John Smart spoke into his radio. "It looks like there are four women and the two drivers in the van."

Harlan replied, "When they leave, get your vehicle and follow us. We will take them down when we get to Mesquite. We've lost the tracker so keep a visual at all time."

"Yes, sir," said Agent Smart.

The van pulled out into the alley and headed for the interstate. We pulled into the alley with our running lights out and began to follow at a safe distance. The knowledge of where they might be headed made the tail easier, and Harlan maneuvered the vehicle with stealth. Once we got on I15, we would fall further back and communicate with the team waiting in Mesquite. We needed to make the bust at the facility they were using to do the surgeries on the girls, and the tail would get tricky when we got closer. We felt confident that we could get one of our vehicles behind the van without raising suspicions and ultimately find the building. Two hours later, the hot desert sun was flashing in our eyes as it rose. The exit signs began to appear for Mesquite.

We edged closer, passing a couple of semitrucks, and easing back three car lengths behind the van. The van signaled and exited on Mesquite Boulevard, and Harlan called it in. There was an unmarked police truck parked in a McDonald's poised to jump in and follow. We slowed and waited for the van to exit the ramp, then shot around a car in front of us and exited in pursuit. As the unmarked police car continued to follow the van down the boulevard, the driver radioed ahead to the second unmarked police car. As the van approached, the second unmarked police car swung into traffic in front of the van. The van driver immediately slowed, and we formed a long law train behind the unsuspecting criminals. A few miles down the road, the van signaled a right-hand turn on East Old Mill Street. The unmarked police car ahead of the van continued straight and would go up a block and turn right, looking for an intersect. We turned right and drove slowly, keeping our distance. The van signaled right again, this time onto Grayson Street. Pulling the Charger over, we called in the turn. The unmarked police car behind us passed us and followed the van. When the driver saw the van turn into a driveway at a purple house at the dead end, he pulled over and called the location in.

*****

Grayson was a dead-end street with modest-sized houses and no sign of any children. The entire block was adjacent to a small casino. It was likely that these homes were occupied by casino employees. We would need to surround the purple house before entering with the SWAT team but would need to warn any other residents at home to stay inside. I said, "Let me go door to door, no one will suspect a woman. I am sure Hassan will have someone watching the street. If anyone questions me, I will tell them I lost my dog and that we both are out looking for him. You can come down to pick me up in your car and take them out!"

"That is too dangerous, Jess," said Harlan. "What if you get shot?"

"Hey, I can handle myself. Just give me a weapon. Something small."

He opened the glove box and pulled out a two-and-a-half-inch Derringer pistol. I slipped it into my jeans at the small of my back and smiled. "Feel better?"

"A little," he said. "Be careful. I will be watching."

I hopped out of the car and began walking slowly down Grayson Street, whistling and calling for my mutt. I went to the door of each house with a car parked in the driveway and carefully explained to the resident what was going on and to stay inside. As I neared the purple house, I heard the sound of a Harley Davidson coming up behind me. You can't miss that engine growl, and I turned to look. The driver pulled his bike into the driveway of the purple house, removed his helmet, and asked in a heavy accent, "Can I be of assistance, miss?"

I immediately explained I had lost my dog and asked if he might have seen it.

"This is an unusual place to lose a dog, miss…?"

"Grant," I said. "Alicia Grant. And you are?

"Kreschev," he replied. "Dr. Vladimir Kreschev."

"It is nice to meet you, sir," I said.

Harlan could hear everything being said, and he whispered into my earpiece, "Kreschev is the owner of the plane! Get out of there now!"

"My husband is helping me look," I said. "He is a block over and will be coming to get me soon."

"Excellent, Mrs. Grant. In the meantime, why don't you come in, and I will ask my wife if she has seen your pet. You look thirsty, and it isn't good to get dehydrated in this hot sun."

"Oh, thank you, but I am fine," I said.

"I don't think so," he said, grabbing my arm viciously, nearly twisting it off. "I think you are a cop. I saw the others when I drove in. You don't know what you have stepped into, my friend, but you are about to find out!"

He shoved me roughly through the front door and shouted for his men.

CHAPTER THIRTY-TWO

Harlan frantically called the team. "They have Jess! The guy on the bike is a Russian! He owns the plane Hassan was flying. He must be the one who implants the drugs in the girls. We have our guy, but he has Jess, so we need a new plan. Get a man over here now to watch the house, and get everyone together in the casino parking lot to figure out how we are going to do this and hurry. We can't let anything happen to Jess, and I mean it!"

Kreschev shoved me into the living room and pointed his gun in my face. "Who are you really?" he snarled.

Alena and three more women sat on the floor in the corner of the room and watched me wide-eyed with terror. Alena lowered her head and shrank into the wall.

"I told you, I'm Alicia Grant. My dog jumped out of the car window a couple blocks from here and ran away. My husband and I are looking for him...that's it!"

"Liar! You are that woman, that coroner from Echo who found Consuela. I am not a stupid man, Ms. DOOGAN! You have interfered with our operations, and you must pay the price." He smiled wickedly and then said, "But before I kill you, you will tell me everything the FBI knows and what their plan is right now. If I am satisfied with the information, I will kill you swiftly. You won't feel a thing. If not..." His henchman then handed him a leather bag, and Kreschev unrolled it slowly, revealing a set of stainless-steel scalpels and knives. I shuddered. "If not, Ms. Doogan, I will cut you slowly into little pieces, starting with your pretty ears." He grabbed my hair and pulled my head back, stuck his thick fingers into my ear, and pulled

73

out the earpiece. He slapped my face hard, drawing blood from my lip. "Did you hear that, Officers? If you want me, it will cost you your woman's life!" he whispered viciously into the earpiece.

CHAPTER THIRTY-THREE

Harlan gathered the SWAT team and FBI together in the casino parking lot. It was early afternoon, so the parking lot was sparsely filled. There was a large ice truck backed into a space near what looked like a utility shed. No one was in the truck, and Harlan brushed off the oddness of its placement and turned to the team. "As you know, they have Jess. I don't think he will kill her now. He needs her to keep us down. I want the SWAT team to surround the house, guns ready, but no firing unless I give the word. I will try to negotiate. The rest of you move your cars to every outlet in case we have to chase and be ready. Let's roll."

It looked like someone had stepped on a bee's nest as the police cars tore out of the parking lot. Harlan and the SWAT team, leading the charge, crossed the parking lot and ran up the grass median to take their places. Harlan took up position directly in front of the house and lifted the bullhorn. "We have you surrounded, Vladimir. There is no way out. Let the girl go, and we can take this to the station. No one needs to die here today!" An agonizing five minutes of silence went by with no response. Harlan spoke again. "Mr. Kreschev, what is it that you want? Just give us the girl, and we can talk about it." Five more minutes of silence, and then the front door opened slightly.

"You!" Kreschev said to Harlan. "Come inside alone. I wish not to have my business broadcast to my neighbors. Just you, and I will give you the girl."

"Send her out first, and I will come in," said Harlan.

"These are not my terms!" Kreschev snarled. "My way or she dies! And leave your weapons."

Harlan's brain was swirling. You train for these situations, but no training could trump the feeling of dread and fear in his heart. The SWAT team was poised and ready to raid at Harlan's call, also fearful of losing one of their own. Harlan removed his ankle gun and handed his service weapon to SWAT. "Okay, I'm coming in." He walked slowly up the steps to the cracked door, eased it open, and stepped inside. The room was empty! "Jess!" he called. "Where are you?" No answer. He opened the door to a bedroom. Nothing! The kitchen, empty! He opened another door into a large room with an operating table, lights, instruments, and IV cart. *This is where they pack the girls*, he thought. "They are gone!" he shouted. The SWAT team entered the house in a flurry, guns up and ready, clearing each room. "There must be a secret way out of here. Check the floors, doors, attic. Everywhere!"

Then a revelation.

"Wait!" Harlan said. "At the dry cleaners, there was a hidden door behind a painting. Maybe, just maybe..." Then he saw it. On the floor in front of the dining-room hutch was a crescent-shaped scratch in the wood. He took both hands, grabbed the edge of the hutch, and pulled it toward him. It opened, revealing a set of stairs. "It's a tunnel. Half of you with me, the rest get ready to drive." They headed down the stairs and began the chase.

CHAPTER THIRTY-FOUR

The utility-shed door in the casino parking lot opened. Manuel slipped out and hurried over to the ice truck. He quickly slid open the back of the truck, revealing an empty bed. Running back to the shed, he grabbed me by the arms, pulling them violently behind me and zip-tying my hands behind my back. He then rushed me out to the truck and violently threw me into the back. My shoulder slammed hard into the metal floor. I felt it dislocate and screamed in pain. Manuel jumped in the truck and quickly slapped duct tape over my mouth, growling, "Shut up, bitch!"

Manuel's partner pushed the four prostitutes that had been held in the tunnel out the door toward us and tossed them into the truck, sending them rolling and whimpering. They knew to make noise was to die, unlike me! Manuel then took a chain and locked the shed door. The two men jumped into the truck and drove casually out of the parking lot.

Meanwhile, on the other side of the parking lot, a wooden hatch opened from the ground in the center of a landscaping effort filled with Joshua trees that lined the parking lot. These trees provided a desert view to the gamblers as well as afforded a small bit of privacy to the residents just yards away. An earthen door lifted up and swung back onto the ground. Vladimir Kreschev emerged, shut the lid, and peered out through the trees. His white minivan was parked just feet away. It was equipped with a child seat in the back, and silhouettes of a family and a cat lined the back window. A bumper sticker with "Honor Roll Student" proudly displayed completed the illusion. He slithered over to the vehicle, unlocked the door, and climbed inside.

Vladimir pulled an auburn wig cut in a long bob style over his nearly bald head and exited the parking lot. Just a soccer mom on her way to pick up the kids.

CHAPTER THIRTY-FIVE

Harlan and his team raced down the stairs into the tunnel. They were nearly fifty yards into it, when they saw the second tunnel running east. "Split up. You guys follow straight, we will take this one. It can't be that far. Move!"

Team one ran straight forward and, in minutes, found themselves climbing a set of stairs into a utility shed. Agent Todd pushed on the door. "Locked," he muttered. He shined a flashlight in the surrounding space and saw shovels, a riding lawn mower, and gas can. The key was in the mower, and without hesitation, he started it up and rammed the vehicle into the door. The wood splintered, and he plowed into it a second time, breaking through to daylight and out onto the casino parking lot. "Wow, these guys thought of everything."

Harlan and his team emerged from the ground on the other end of the parking lot and stepped into view. Scouring the parking lot, he remarked, "There was a truck parked by that shed, I remember! I thought it was odd. It was an ice truck. Put an APB out on a twenty-foot ice truck, white with blue letters, probably heading north. It looks like they split up. My bet is Kreschev is alone, and the truck has Jess and the girls. They have a good fifteen-minute lead on us. Get the cars and cover every street you can."

CHAPTER THIRTY-SIX

Inside the back of the truck, a single beam of pale light from the ventilation fan on the top of the truck pierced the darkness and lit a small circle in the middle of the floor. It was enough light for me to see the shadows of the women in the corner. I struggled furiously, trying to free my hands. It was excruciating, with my injured shoulder bringing tears to my eyes and nearly causing me to pass out from the pain. The blood from my lip had soaked through the duct tape, and I could feel the duct tape loosening around my lips. Kissing furiously and pushing with my tongue, I was able to free my mouth to speak. I called out in the dark for Alena. "There is a knife in my left pocket. Get it out and cut my ties. I am frightened. They will kill us all for this, I know!"

"Don't be afraid, Alena. I have a plan. Harlan will find us, everything is going to be fine. Please get my knife. We have to get out of this. Please, Alena, please." Alena slowly crawled over blindly, feeling for my body. When she found me, she reached into my pocket and quickly got my knife.

"Try not to cut me," I said.

"To be sure," she said, and gently maneuvered the knife blade under the zip tie and began to carefully saw the plastic. In moments, my hands fell free. I reached down the back of my jeans with my good arm and pulled the Derringer out. It was fully loaded and ready to fire. Now all we could do was wait.

A half hour passed when the truck rolled to a stop, and we heard the passenger door open. Someone punched in some numbers on a keypad, and we heard the sound of a large metal door on a chain open. The truck drove slowly in, and the door closed with a heavy clunk behind us. We could hear the men walking around the truck to the back. I positioned myself on one knee, with the gun pointed at the closed door.

The moment Manuel pulled up on the back door and his body came into view, I shot him, hitting him squarely in the chest and knocking him to the ground. His partner started to run, and I fired a shot into his back, sending him sprawling. "Get the zip ties out of the truck and tie these guys' hands and feet!" I shouted to the girls in the truck. They looked terrified but did as I asked. Manuel was bleeding profusely, desperately crawling across the floor. I leaped on his back, straddling him, and tied his hands. Then, just for spite, I took the roll of duct tape and wrapped a tight circle around his head and mouth. *You might consider shaving your head after we pull this off your face, you pig. Ha!*

Both men were alive but unconscious and bleeding profusely. I took their guns and patted them down. In Manuel's pocket I found a cell phone and quickly dialed Harlan's number. He picked up on the first ring, snarling, "Who is this?"

"Harlan, it's me! We are in some garage about thirty minutes from the casino. I have no idea what direction we went, but it is a big metal building, and it looks like it might have been a service garage for big trucks. There is a lift on the floor in one of the bays, it is greasy and smells like garbage."

"Jess, thank God! Are you all right?"

"We are fine. I shot the two men who took us. They are alive and contained but will need an ambulance. Kreschev is not with them."

"Hang tight, Jess. Leave the cell phone on, we can find you with GPS. We're on our way." Harlan quickly described the location on his radio, and the local LEOs immediately knew the place. Thank God for the Mesquite Police Department! They gave Harlan the address and sped toward the garage.

CHAPTER THIRTY-SEVEN

Kreschev pulled the minivan into the warehouse yard and drove up to the keypad. He entered the numbers.

We heard the big door start to open and a car door slam shut. I positioned myself just inside the door on the right with the 9 mm pistol taken from the driver. As the minivan nosed into the garage, Kreschev turned his head and saw me standing with the gun raised. He threw the vehicle into reverse and gunned it. I leaped out and fired three shots into his van. One broke the windshield and another nicked a front tire and blew a hole through his side mirror. He tore out of the driveway and started heading south just as three MPD cars roared in with Harlan right behind them in the Charger. "Keep him alive!" shouted Harlan.

The cops fired into all four tires, crippling the vehicle, and Kreschev rolled to a stop. "Out of the car with your hands on your head!" shouted an officer. "Kreschev eased out of the driver's seat and stood on the road as ordered. Harlan raced over to Kreschev and cuffed him, read him his rights, roughly dragged him into the garage, and shoved him hard onto the desk chair in the small office in the far corner of the room. There was a laptop and printer on the desk and a small safe on the floor between two filing cabinets. An officer kept his gun pointed at Kreschev as Harlan began tearing into the cabinets. He found nothing but auto-repair invoices and service records. Turning to Kreschev, he demanded the combination to the safe. The officer's gun on Kreschev's kneecap was enough encouragement to get the numbers, and Harlan quickly punched in the code, and the door popped open. Inside was a small wooden box with a keylock. "Where is the key? Give it to me now!"

"I don't know what you are talking about, I know nothing of any key. I have never seen this box."

"'Liar! Search him, check his pockets, I know he has it."

The officer did as he was told and quickly found the small key enclosed in Kreschev's wallet. He handed it to Harlan while Kreschev turned his head in defeat.

The key slipped easily into the box, and Harlan carefully lifted the lid. *Liquid heroin,* just as I thought.

"Take this cretin to the station and book him. Assault with a deadly weapon, drug trafficking, anything else you can think of. Just get him out of my sight. FBI will take over the case when we get this sorted out. Just lock him up and throw away the key," he told the officer. "In the meantime, the rest of you secure the scene. This is a big fish, gentlemen, thank you!"

Ambulances were on the way, and a patrolman was assuring the four frightened prostitutes that everything would be fine.

I stood in the doorway, smiling weakly, as Harlan rushed over and pulled me into his arms, squeezing me tight. I yelled out in pain and he pulled back. "What happened? You're hurt!" I explained my shoulder injury, and he handed me a handkerchief to wipe the blood from my lip and face.

"You are lucky to be alive, Jess. You took out two guys with that pistol! That is amazing."

"It's a Derringer. What can I say?" I laughed.

"We have to get you to the hospital right now and get that shoulder looked at," Harlan said seriously.

Just then the ambulance arrived. We led them to the two wounded criminals lying facedown on the floor. They were loaded onto the gurneys and into the ambulance with a police escort and lights flashing. Alena and the three other girls were loaded into the back of another patrol car to be taken downtown for questioning and held for the FBI. Harlan gently helped me into his car, and we headed for the emergency room.

CHAPTER THIRTY-EIGHT

The doctor set my shoulder, and I screamed in pain. Harlan squeezed my hand. God that hurt! I braved a smile and jokingly said to the doc, "Do I get a discount for pain and suffering?" He laughed and told me I would be fine in a few weeks, to get plenty of rest and handed me a prescription for painkillers. We picked it up in the hospital pharmacy, and I immediately popped two into my mouth and chased them down with water from the fountain in the lobby. "Where to now?" I asked Harlan.

"I'm taking you back to your hotel, and you are going to bed. You did good, Jess, real good. I am proud of you."

The drugs were kicking in as we drove south back to Vegas. We rehashed the events of the past few days, laughing now at the amazing trip down the river and the extraordinary twists and turns this case had delivered. It felt good to laugh, and I fought the urge to slide over and kiss that handsome FBI guy right on the lips. He was driving after all, so that probably wasn't smart. So I didn't. I just closed my eyes and let the prescription take me away.

An hour later, I felt a nudge on my arm. "Jess, we're here. C'mon, I will take you to your room. Can you walk okay?"

I giggled. "Oooooh, yes. I can walk, I can talk, I can rope, I can ride, and I'm a badass ME with an attitude, baby!"

"I think the drugs are working just fine." Harlan chuckled. He half-carried me up to my room and unlocked the door, led me inside, and sat me gently on the bed.

"You can join me," I said, slurring my words and staring at five Harlans looking back at me.

"In time, baby," he said seductively. "In time. You need to get some sleep. Agent Todd will pick you up in the morning and take you to the airport. You can recover at home, and we can debrief you later. Just get some rest." He paused. "You know, I have some vacation time coming, and if you're up to it, I sure would like to learn how to rope. Do you think you could teach me?"

I smiled at him. "Ya know, Mr. Harlan Meeks, if you want to rope with the big girls, your gonna have to learn to ride!" I gave him my most sensuous smile and then burst out laughing. "Saddle up, baby."

He flashed his brilliant white smile, bent down, and kissed me deeply on the mouth. I melted. "Have a safe trip home, and I'll call you." He gently laid me back on the bed, kissed my forehead, and shut the door softly behind him as he left.

CHAPTER THIRTY-NINE

Harlan picked up his phone and called Director Todd in Vegas. "We have SWAT and an investigative team in Mesquite clearing the crime scene and looking for drugs. Take the dry cleaners now. Look for someone named Hassan. He is apparently second in command. I think we have it, Geoff, finally!"

Todd ordered the move, and a swarm of FBI agents broke through the doors front and back of the dry cleaners. Inside they arrested three women who looked like deer in headlights and headed to the basement where they found the ugly Russian grunt stuffing money into a bag and heading toward the staircase. He was tackled and subdued quickly by one of the detectives. Upon searching him, they found a small key with "LV1" stamped on the face. "What does this open, comrade?" The detective pushed the barrel of his gun into the Russian's mouth. The Russian's eyes told him where to look. The bookcase was filled with an unusual number of paperbacks. Who keeps them after all? The detective began tossing the books off the shelf and revealed a wall safe. He took the LV1 key and slipped it into the cylinder. It turned and, upon opening, revealed rows of plastic canisters identical to the ones found in the girls, at least a dozen. "Score, you're busted," announced the detective. Putting the Russian's hands behind his back, the detective cuffed him and called in the find to agent Todd. Todd replied immediately. "This is good," Todd said. "We found a safe with a lockbox filled with the drugs in Mesquite as well. The key was numbered MQ2. It appears they have a number of distribution points for the girls. So far, they are somehow tied to casinos. Let's check into Colorado and see if we can figure out why these girls were being transported there in the first place. It will have to be tribal. Look in southern Colorado first then check the metro areas Colorado Springs and Denver. It could even be in New Mexico for that matter. Leave nothing to chance. Call the tribal police in all those areas and find out if there is a heroin problem springing up. We are close, men. We are close."

CHAPTER FORTY

Hassan slipped out of his suite and took the service elevator at Caesars down the twenty-nine flights to the parking garage. He put on his helmet, climbed onto the Ducati, and drove out onto the strip. He knew the airplane would be confiscated, the airport heavily guarded, and police everywhere looking for him. On his bike under a helmet, he would be less likely to be stopped by law enforcement. As far as he knew, no one knew what he looked like by photo, just descriptions from his traitorous employees, perhaps they fabricated his likeness or not, but he intended to keep his image a ghost. It would be at least five hours to Ignacio. He would meet with Black Hawk at the Raven Feather Casino and devise a plan. There was over a million dollars' worth of pure heroin in the lockbox hidden there as well as the six women Manuel had delivered earlier. He hoped by now the drugs had been removed from them. This should be enough to start operations again and reestablish the pipeline. He had to get that key. The question was, did the FBI have it or was it lost in the river? As he roared down the highway, he formulated his plan. He would kidnap the medical examiner, a woman no less, who destroyed his empire and get the information he needed. Then he would cut her into pieces and mail her back to the FBI. The thought made him laugh out loud.

Up ahead on the desert, he could see the prairie dogs sunning themselves in the blazing sun. He turned the Ducati off the pavement and drove out onto the crusted earth, dodging sagebrush and flagstone as the dust blew a tornado behind him. He parked the bike in the minimal shade of a scrub oak tree and reached into his saddle-bag for the .357 Magnum, his favorite pistol.

He heard the rattle before he saw the snake. A six-foot diamondback lay curled under the oak, head raised, rattle shaking, and poised to strike. Hassan whirled and shot the snake, the bullet ripping its head from its body and watched it writhe as death caught up with it. Seconds passed, and the snake was still. Hassan took his jagged-edge bowie knife and sawed the remains off the head of his prey. *Perfect*, he thought. He stepped out from behind the tree and scoured the horizon for prairie dogs. In moments, a curious rodent raised his head from its hole, and Hassan's shot removed it. He walked over to the den, picked up the dead dog, and carried it back to his bike. He pried open the snake's mouth and impaled the prairie dog into its fangs and then carefully put the snakehead and dead prairie dog into a Carl's Jr. bag leftover from a lunch stop from who knows how long ago. Later he would transfer this to a box and send Ms. Doogan a very special gift. He fired up the Ducati and headed toward Ignacio.

CHAPTER FORTY-ONE

It was ten the next morning when Agent Todd knocked on my hotel-room door. I was not in near the pain I had experienced the day before, and my head was clear. I opened the door, and he stepped in with a couple of Starbucks' coffees in hand. Handing me mine, he said, "Jess, you have proven yourself to be a very valuable asset to the FBI. If you would consider it, we would like to have you join our team permanently. You would need training, of course, and the bureau would pay to send you to Quantico for eighteen weeks. With your skills, you should pass without a hitch, and we will be waiting for you. How does that sound?"

I sat staring back at him in disbelief. "Can I think about it?"

"Of course, you can. The next session at the academy starts in a month. Get healed up, and let me know what you decide in, say, three weeks. Will that work for you?"

I swallowed a sip of my coffee and looked him straight in the eye. "Yes, sir, I believe I can have an answer for you by then, and thank you for the opportunity!"

"All right then," he said. "Let's get you home."

We left the hotel and drove to the plane waiting for us on the tarmac. I boarded, and we took off for my Colorado home.

*****

My plane touched down in Cortez at 2:00 p.m. Dad was there to pick me up, and we embraced warmly. I was happy to be home and still whirling from the wild couple of days' incredible activity.

On the two-hour drive back up to Echo, I told Ben about Agent Todd's offer to send me to Quantico and watched his stoic expression as he drove in silence. "C'mon, Dad, you know I can handle myself. You taught me everything I know. If you had a chance like this when you were my age, you know you would have been all over it!"

"Jess," he said, "you could have been killed on that river. I don't even want to know what happened in Nevada to you. And look, you are all I have, kid. When we lost your mother, I swore I would never let anything bad happen to you. This FBI nonsense is too dangerous. Please. Think about your future. Maybe get married, have some kids. I would like grandchildren. We could teach them to cowboy. It is a dying art. Just think about it, Jess. That's all I ask."

We continued on in silence until arriving at my cabin. "Okay, Dad, I will think about it."

He nodded approvingly and said, "I invited a few of your friends over tomorrow for a barbecue and birthday party for you. Told everyone to come by about five."

In all the craziness of the last few days, I had completely forgotten my birthday. I smiled and said, "Absolutely, Dad, that would be great. Thank you!"

We pulled up to my house, I gave him a hug and climbed out of the truck, went up the three steps to my cabin door, and stepped inside. Everything was just as I left it. Clothes scattered everywhere, dirty dishes in the sink. I sighed and resigned myself to the mess that no one but me would clean.

CHAPTER FORTY-TWO

From his suite at the Raven Feather, Hassan carefully packed his morbid snakehead creation with a handprinted one-word note, "Die," for Jess, in a FedEx overnight express box and addressed it to "Medical Examiner, Fogerty Funeral Home Echo, Colorado." He would deliver it himself. There could be no more mistakes, and he wanted to see the shock and fear on her face when she opened it. He packed a duffel bag with his rifle, ammunition, a black hooded sweatshirt, and gloves, and he left the casino and walked three blocks to the Hertz car rental. He rented a midsize Toyota, silver and common, with a good-sized trunk. If this Jess didn't have his key, he would use her as leverage.

CHAPTER FORTY-THREE

I took a hot shower, made a cup of tea, and curled up in my recliner with a copy of *Tactical Response* magazine. I was excited about training for the FBI even without Dad's full approval. He would come around. I would talk with him more tomorrow.

My thoughts were interrupted by the phone ring. I thought about letting the machine get it and then rose and went to the desk and picked up. It was Harlan. "Jess, glad you're home safely. I wanted to give you an update on the case. We were able to connect with the Portugese ambassador and arrange to extradite the bodies of the four victims to their families. I will be flying in the day after tomorrow to pick up Consuela from you. Can you get her ready for transport?"

"Of course," I replied. "I can have Russ Fogerty, our funeral director, prepare the body and pick out a casket for her. She deserves a dignified return to her family."

We talked a few more minutes and said good night. I would call Russ in the morning and help with Consuela. I hadn't been back to my lab for days and had left everything in a hurry. It would be just like my house, a mess to clean up, but for now, I was going to shut it all out and get some sleep.

CHAPTER FORTY-FOUR

The morning sun cast ribbons of warm light through the window as I crawled out of bed. This was my favorite part of the day with birds singing as the air warmed and the constant color change as the sky turned from orange to blue. I ground up a bold French roast and put it in the press, poured a cup, stepped out onto the deck, and sat on my swing. Today would be busy, and my first order of business was to call Russ and then go shopping. Consuela needed something nice to be buried in, and the local clothing shop in Echo, though small in variety, should have something appropriate. And what the heck, it was my birthday; maybe I would get myself some new digs. Harlan would be here tomorrow, and I knew I could make a better impression. I made arrangements with Russ to meet at noon and headed downtown.

Rachel's Rags and Mercantile was Echo's version of a department store slash farm supply. The townsfolk supported her well, and she did her best to keep a nice variety of the latest fashions to go with your muck boots and manure rakes. I pulled up to the front and parked. In the front window display was a mannequin dressed in a pair of cowgirl jeans, ostrich-skin boots, and beautiful red peasant blouse with a jeweled bodice. Perfect, I thought! I went in and bought the blouse. I picked one up for myself in a deep lapis blue and got a pair of black jeans to go with it. I paid the clerk and left for my lab.

Jess didn't notice the silver Toyota parked up the street from Rachel's when she left. Hassan made a U-turn and slowly followed her truck as she headed toward the funeral home. He would tail her today and learn all he needed, then tonight he would make his move.

CHAPTER FORTY-FIVE

I unlocked the door to my lab. It would be an hour before Russ got here, and there was plenty for me to do. The lab was cold. I turned on the lights, turned up the thermostat. My instruments were scattered across the tables, and there was dried mud everywhere. I went to the broom closet and got the mop bucket, broom, dustpan, and a sponge. The dried mud turned to dust under the bristles. Releasing the wheels on my exam table, I pushed it out a foot to sweep when I saw the key. I went to the drawer, put on rubber gloves and carefully picked it up. It was a small key with "C3" engraved in it. There were no teeth in the key, it looked just like the one we had found in Mesquite. How could I have missed this! I carefully put the key in an evidence bag and placed it in a box on the filing cabinet. Harlan would be here tomorrow, and I would give it to him then. I took my frustration out on the floors as I finished cleaning, and they shone like mirrors as a result.

Russ arrived right at noon, and we removed Consuela from the vault. He would do the embalming. While he did that, I went to the showroom and selected a simple white casket with a pink silk lining to lay her to rest. She would look beautiful in her red blouse. The FBI would compensate Fogerty's for all this, and I was grateful and proud of them for the extra effort made toward the families of these poor girls.

It was nearly 3:00 p.m. when we finished. I thanked Russ for his kindness, and we locked up and left. I would go home quickly and change into my new outfit and head over to Dad's. I wanted to tell him about the key I had found before the other guests arrived.

The silver Toyota pulled out of the cemetery and slowly followed Jess.

CHAPTER FORTY-SIX

I pulled into my driveway and ran into the cabin, quickly changed clothes, grabbed a warm jacket as nights were still pretty chilly, and I wasn't sure if Dad was doing the guitar jam around the bonfire or if we were staying inside. Either way, it would be fun, and I looked forward to a birthday shot and a beer. Half an hour later, I pulled up to Ben's sprawling ranch. He had one of the most coveted views that included the tip of Lone Cone volcano always capped with snow and a hundred acres of green pasture with Echo Creek snaking its way through the fields and flowing into the huge spring-fed pond that Dad kept stocked with trout. It was a postcard. As I pulled into the huge circular drive and up to his fabulous log home, Bodie's patrol car along with two other vehicles were already there. Our key discussion would have to wait. I hopped out of the truck and entered the soiree.

CHAPTER FORTY-SEVEN

Hassan pulled the Toyota around to the back of Jess's cabin and stepped out. There was a small storage shed in the back and an abandoned doghouse. Grateful for the dog's absence, he continued to peruse the yard and made his way to the back door of the cabin. Jess had no neighbors nearby, so he felt confident no one would see him. He tried the door and, to his delight, found it unlocked. He slipped inside. The cabin was quaint with a small kitchen, a wood stove on a stone hearth in one corner, living room with a whiskey barrel that served as a lamp table next to a cowhide sofa, and surprisingly, no television to be found. There was a door off the living room that led to her bedroom, which had a large window overlooking an aspen grove. Her master bathroom was small with a shower only and small linen closet. A second bathroom and laundry room was off the kitchen. He would hide there and attack her from behind. *Where would the bitch hide the key?* he thought. He first checked her jewelry box then looked in all the drawers. There was a desk with a filing cabinet, which he went carefully through file by file. Her computer was password protected, but he didn't care what was on it anyway. This woman had disrupted and nearly destroyed their drug-trafficking operation, and he could care less who her friends on Facebook were. Finding nothing anywhere, it could only mean she had already turned it over as evidence, or it wasn't on Consuela's body when they found her. Either way, Jess Doogan was going to die. He carefully placed the "gift box" outside the front door and went back inside, picked up the magazine Jess had been reading, and sat down on the sofa to wait.

CHAPTER FORTY-EIGHT

The party roared on at Ben's well after dark, but the harsh wind denied us the bonfire option. Instead we gabbed and giggled, told tales, and relaxed indoors. Nearly everyone at the party had been touched in some way by the crazy events of the last week, and getting back to the normal laid-back fun of mountain country living was a welcome relief to all of us. I was cajoled and poked at for being past my prime as a breeding mare by a few of the guys whose asses I had whooped on the rifle range and rodeo grounds many a time, but it was all in fun and took me out of my intense headset of the past few days. I was even a little tipsy, if the truth be known! I decided to keep the key find under my hat and let the night be what it was. *Fun.* I thanked everyone for coming, gave Dad a hug, and made my way out to my truck. It was all back roads home, and I already knew Bodie would give me a pass. The worst that could happen would be an elk or deer jumping into my path, and I wasn't planning on speeding home anyway.

There were a bazillion stars in the sky with a sliver of a moon casting a ribbon of light across the road. I was thirty-five years old, single, living in the middle of nowhere basically, but somehow incredibly happy. Even more so now that Harlan had swooped into my life. God, I liked him. I also loved the excitement and intrigue of discovering the answers to the man-made mysteries that crime provided. I knew in my heart I would tell Agent Todd I was in!

My cabin porch light came into view as I rounded the curve. Home. I pulled up to the front porch and parked. I had left the porch light on and could see a FedEx package at the door. Maybe a surprise birthday gift, ooh, I loved surprises. I reached down for the package and saw it was addressed to my lab. *That's weird*, I thought. Unlocking the front door, I entered and strode over to the kitchen counter to get a knife and see what this little package was. There was no return address, so I hadn't a clue what it was or even where it came from. I pulled a paring knife from the block and cut the tape. Whatever it was, it was wrapped in white gauze, and I could clearly see the bloodstains. I took the knife and began a careful cut across the top of the gauze, and it fell to the sides, revealing a hideous snake with a faceless creature in its mouth and a single word on a Post-it note: DIE! I screamed, leaped back in horror, and heard the gun hammer click behind me. I whipped around to face my enemy. "Who are you, and what do you want?" I stammered. The man was small, maybe five feet tall at most, and his face had a jagged scar from the top of his head across his left eye and over his lip. His eyelid hung loosely over his left eye, and half of his head was covered with stringy black hair scantily combed over the scar.

"You have something of mine, Ms. Doogan, and you will give it to me now!" the man said.

"I don't know what you are talking about. Who are you?" I pleaded.

"I am Hassan," he hissed. "You have made things very difficult for me, and now you must pay. The head of the snake is just one part, my dear, but the poison can still kill. You will give me my key now!"

I leaped toward the counter for the knife, Hassan fired a shot into the box, and the snake splattered next to me. I froze.

"Never bring a knife to a gunfight." He smirked. "Now! Give me the key."

"It isn't here," I said.

"Too bad for you then, Ms. Doogan. You will die slowly. I will cut your fingers off one at a time and listen to you scream, then I will cut off your ears, cut out your eyes, and finally your tongue. This will be my gift to the FBI! Or you will give me the key, and I will put a bullet between your eyes, and you will feel nothing. The choice is yours," he said with a sinister grin.

My mind was whirling. This man was insane! "The key is in my lab," I finally said.

Hassan forced me to the ground at gunpoint and zip-tied my hands behind my back. He grabbed my car keys, which had my office key on the ring, went outside to his car where he opened the trunk, and shoved me inside. He slammed the trunk shut and peeled out of the driveway toward Fogerty's.

CHAPTER FORTY-NINE

The Toyota pulled into the rear parking lot of Fogerty's funeral home, and I heard the car door slam shut and Hassan's footfalls as he came to the trunk. I was afraid to make any sudden moves as he had proven himself unafraid to use his gun. He opened the trunk and pulled me out by my arms, and I groaned in pain from my still very sore shoulder. He shoved me forward, and we went to the door. He took my keys and let us in.

"I need my hands so I can get the key. There is a knife in the drawer, and the key is locked in the safe," I said.

He cut me free and pushed me toward the safe; the gun was in the small of my back, pressing hard. I bent over to the safe lock and began to dial the combination. I could hear Hassan's breathing speeding up through his crooked nose. His face was peering over my shoulder when I swung back hard with my elbow, catching him on the chin and knocking him off balance. I turned swiftly and placed a foot deep into his groin, and he fell forward and the gun hit the floor and flew from his hands, slamming into the steel-body vault. I followed the groin kick with an equal slam of my foot into his face, grabbed his .357, and ran out the door. Racing to the car, I opened the door only to find the keys were not in the ignition. I had no choice but to run and took off furiously into the cemetery to hide.

Hassan angrily shook his head and tried to rise. His throbbing groin inhibited his effort, and he cursed aloud as he jerked to his feet and weaved out the door to find Jess. His car door was open, and she was nowhere in sight. He peered into the darkness and saw the gravestones. She had to be there. Pulling his loaded rifle from the floor of the back seat, he grabbed a box of ammo and raced up into the cemetery.

I ran blindly through the headstones in the cemetery, looking for something large enough to get behind and watch from. Ahead I saw it. A six-foot-tall angel towered above the grave. I slipped in behind her base and sat with my back leaning against her, praying that I could get out of this alive. The .357 was clutched in my hand, and I rolled open the cylinder. Three bullets remained in the gun.

From a short distance away, I could hear the angry footfalls of Hassan as he stumbled through the graveyard, looking. He yelled out, "You are a dead woman, there is no escape. Show yourself!"

I took a deep breath and tried to think. I could hear him but not see him. I wasn't sure if he had a weapon but bet he was armed with something. I needed a distraction. On the ground right next to me was a broken flowerpot. The wind had probably blown it from its place on the headstone. I picked it up and flung it as far as my arm could throw, and it crashed into another headstone. The shot rang out and ricocheted. I had seen the fire and now knew where Hassan was. I watched as he slowly crept toward the area and could barely see his shadow in the scant moonlight. I aimed the .357 as best I could and fired. Missed! Hassan shouted out, laughing. "You must be better than that, Ms. Doogan. You only have two shots left. I have thirty. Appropriate we are in a graveyard, for here you will remain."

I ran as quietly as I could, weaving in and out of the head-stones as shots fired behind me. There was a gravel path ahead that would lead me back around to the automobile entrance to the cemetery lined with trees. If I could get back to my office, I could lock myself in and call for help. A shot hit a tree right next to me, and I stopped. Hassan was barely visible, and I could see the flashing lights of a police car roaring up to the funeral home. Someone must have heard the gunfire and called it in. Thank God! It was now or never. He was fifty yards away. I made that shot a million times on the range. I stepped out from behind the tree and fired. Hassan fell to the ground clutching his stomach and screaming in pain. A gut shot. He could bleed out if not taken care of quickly. I ran toward the upcoming police car, waving my arms. Bodie was at the wheel and quickly stopped.

"Call an ambulance!" I shouted. "I have shot Hassan. He is in the cemetery about one hundred yards in off the drive. We need to keep him alive!" I jumped into the car with Bodie, and he radioed for the ambulance as we roared up the drive toward Hassan. He was unconscious and bleeding heavily. We administered what little first aid we could to him, secured the rifle, and waited for the ambulance to arrive. Fifteen minutes went by when we heard the sirens and saw the flashing lights. They could see our headlights and drove quickly to the spot, put Hassan on the gurney, and rushed him into the vehicle and life support. They would stabilize him at the tiny rural Echo hospital and move him to Cortez when and if he survived. He would require an armed guard, and we notified the Cortez PD to have a man available to us and followed the ambulance to the hospital.

In all the chaos of the evening, I had been oblivious to myself, and as we entered the emergency room behind Hassan, a nurse ushered me into an exam room and began cleaning the dried blood from my face. I had a small cut and huge bruise on my cheek where he had shoved me into the trunk, hitting the spare tire. My healing dislocated shoulder throbbed from having my hands tied behind my back, and my knees felt weak as the adrenaline rush subsided. Harlan would be here in the morning, and everything will be all right. *Dad is going to love this!* I thought. And then I blacked out.

On the operating table, surgeons worked furiously, trying to keep Hassan alive. The heart monitor beeped slower and slower then flatlined. They pulled out the paddles and tried to restart his heart, but to no avail. Hassan Ahmadi was dead.

CHAPTER FIFTY

I opened my eyes and slowly looked around. I was in a hospital bed attached to an IV. I didn't remember anything after arriving at the hospital the night before. A nurse came in and smiled at me. "You had quite a night, Jess," she said. The stress you were under coupled with severe dehydration you suffered was too much for you. You have been sleeping steadily for the last ten hours."

"What time is it? Where is Hassan?" Before she could answer, Ben Doogan entered the room and came to my side. He took my hand and said, "You scared me, kid."

"I'm fine, Dad, really I am. I shot him. I shot Hassan."

"No, Jess, you killed him. He died on the table last night. FBI has been notified, and Harlan should be here in about an hour. I think you should leave this up to them now, Jess. Please, kid!" he implored.

"I can't do that, Dad. We have come too far, and I am going to see this through, you have to trust me."

Ben smiled weakly and resigned. "I am proud of you, Jess, and your mom would be too. Now go finish this."

Harlan arrived at the hospital just as they were releasing me. We embraced, and it felt good. I told him everything that had happened and about finding the key. He told me that there were keys found in the other locations and what they were for. "They are special digitally programmed keys that open the lockboxes. Very high-tech. Each had a number on it, and I need to see what the one you have says. They appear to indicate a location."

We went to my lab, and I got the key for him. It was clearly marked C3, indicating *Colorado* for the place and *three* for the box number. Where in Colorado was the question. Where had Hassan come from?

We ran the license plate on Hassan's vehicle and discovered it to be a rental originating in Ignacio, Colorado. The Raven Feather Casino was there, and that made sense as so far every bust had a casino involved. The Raven Feather was owned by the Ute tribe and would require their permission and cooperation to investigate. Harlan made the calls and initiated the process. Consuela would have to wait a few more days. We were going to Ignacio.

CHAPTER FIFTY-ONE

The Raven Feather Casino loomed large up ahead as we entered the small town of Ignacio. Our first stop would be at the rental-car office to confirm Hassan's identity. We learned that he rented the vehicle under the name Franklin Ferote. We had his wallet and discovered four different driver's licenses all with aliases. We would use these photos to find out if he had checked in at the casino, and we made our way over to the Casino hotel.

The young woman behind the counter at the hotel looked at the photo on the license as we asked her if this man had checked in to the hotel before. She looked uncomfortable and told us she would be unable to answer that but would get the casino manager to speak with us. A few minutes later, a very large Native American man—with long black hair braided on each side of his face tied with leather bands and feathers hanging—opened the door and invited us into his office. He introduced himself as Roland Black Hawk, executive director of casino operations. Roland sat quietly and listened as we described the events of the last five days. His face showed no emotion. He examined the photo of Hassan and said, "This man, Franklin, he is a high roller here and comes often. He spends thousands of dollars and leaves excellent tips. I find it hard to believe he is the person you described."

"Well, Mr. Black Hawk, Franklin was just one of his aliases, and apparently he chose to be a nice person using this one. I can assure you he was a horrible, evil man who did unthinkable things to women and animals. Having him dead is a good thing for everyone, and hopefully we will find the contraband we are looking for in his room," said Harlan.

Black Hawk replied, "I will take you to it immediately. The Raven Feather cannot afford bad publicity, and this could have serious ramifications to our business. I would appreciate your confidentiality on the subject. Tribal police will join you in his room to oversee the collection of evidence."

We thanked him, shook hands, and he escorted us to the service elevators where we rode to Hassan's penthouse suite.

Two armed tribal officers were waiting at the door to Hassan's room. They opened the door, and we entered. There was a motorcycle helmet and leathers neatly placed on the bed, a roll of packing tape and a Sharpie pen on the counter, and nothing else. Hassan had obviously spent little time here. Black Hawk watched quietly as we bagged the items then spoke. "The safe is in this closet." He opened the closet door and punched in the code to open the safe. Harlan reached into the safe and pulled out a wooden box. He set the box on the counter, removed the key from the evidence bag, and inserted it into the lock. The lid popped open instantly, and inside was a dozen three-ounce canisters filled with the liquid heroin. "This is exactly what we found in Vegas and Mesquite," remarked Harlan. "We estimate at least three million dollars on the street. Thank you for your cooperation, Mr. Black Hawk." We shook hands with all the men, gathered the evidence, and left the Raven Feather for Echo.

*****

Roland Black Hawk watched through the window as we drove away. Picking up the phone, he dialed the reservation medical clinic and asked to speak with Dr. Robani. They would begin operations again with the heroin in the six women all waiting for extraction. By tomorrow, they would be back in business!

CHAPTER FIFTY-TWO

The drive back to Echo was a blur as Harlan and I talked endlessly over the case. It had been frightening, invigorating, and life changing for me, and having this wonderful man coming into my life was almost more than I could believe. We would get the drugs to headquarters, return the dead girls to their waiting families, and I would tell Agent Todd to sign me up for Quantico, but for now I slid over close to Harlan, and he put his arm around my shoulder. We were going home.

ABOUT THE AUTHOR

Keri Mills was born and raised in the Eastern Upper Peninsula of Michigan. This Newberry "Yooper" earned her Bachelor of Fine Arts Degree from Central Michigan University and went on to enjoy a successful career in radio advertising. For over thirty years, Keri has written, produced, and sold award-winning thirty- and sixty-second commercials for business owners in Utah and the Pacific Northwest. She is still actively writing and producing ads for clients from her rustic ranch home in the San Juan Mountains of Colorado.

Keri's love of words, vivid imagination, and creativity made adventuring into book writing a natural transition. *Coyote Justice* is her first book in a planned series.

CPSIA information can be obtained
at www.ICGtesting.com
Printed in the USA
FSHW021430020320
67601FS